Praise for *North*

"Author Joan Livingston takes the reader to the heart of the *Northern Comfort* community. The hardship comes through in every carefully placed word as the tragic tale unfolds. A great read that will stay with me."

Paula R C Readman
Author of *The Funeral Birds, Stone Angels, Seeing the Dark*, and *The Phoenix Hour*

"*Northern Comfort* is a stunning, bittersweet tale of broken hearts and broken lives."

Gary Kruse,
Author of *Badlands* and *Bleak Waters*

"*Northern Comfort* is reminiscent of *Grapes of Wrath*, minus the migrant workers and drought. Both paint a picture of harsh life of rural poverty in America. I found *Northern Comfort* a story of tragedy along with a bit of triumph. It showed the strength in people who we sometimes think don't have it in them. And as I said, there is triumph as people make the best of their life, especially Willi and Miles — a relationship born out of tragedy. Beautifully written, its setting and characters last long after the book is closed. If you shut your eyes, you feel the winter chill and freeze in your bones, and see the little town and all it offers, or doesn't, as the case may be. A 5 Star Must Read and another winner from author Joan Livingston."

Joseph Lewis,
Author of Fan Mail

"Heart-wrenching and atmospheric! Livingston masterfully sets the stage for a beautifully told dark drama that will pull on your every heartstring."

JD Spero,
Author of *The Secret Cure*

"Compelling, big-hearted and poignant. Northern Comfort is an acutely observed portrait of small town life."

Michelle Cook,
Author of Tipping Point and Counterpoint.

Northern Comfort

Joan Livingston

DARK
STROKE

www.darkstroke.com

Discover us online:
www.darkstroke.com

Find us on instagram:
www.instagram.com/darkstrokebooks

Include **#darkstroke** in a photo of yourself
holding this book on Instagram and
something nice will happen.

For Karen Westergaard and Victor Morrill

About the Author

Joan Livingston is the author of novels for adult and young readers, including the *Isabel Long Mystery Series*. For *The Sacred Dog* and *Northern Comfort*, she relies on her deep knowledge of rural Western Massachusetts, where she lives and once covered as a long-time journalist, to create realistic characters and settings.

For more, visit her website: **www.joanlivingston.net**. Follow her on Twitter **@joanlivingston**, Instagram **@JoanLivingston_Author**, and TikTok **@joanlivingston_author.** Her author page on Facebook: **www.facebook.com/JoanLivingstonAuthor/**

Acknowledgements

I continue to extend my appreciation to those who have encouraged me to write, as well as those who read my books. In many cases, they are the same. I am especially grateful for the support of my husband, Hank, and our family.

I would like to express my gratitude to the maple sugarers I interviewed when I was a reporter many years ago, especially Paul Sena, who still carries on that tradition in the Western Massachusetts hilltown of Worthington.

Thanks to Chris Mirakian, who was the first one to put eyes on Northern Comfort. And a special thanks to my publishers, Laurence and Steph Patterson, of darkstroke books, who have shown continued faith in my writing. Laurence also edited this novel — a thoroughly enjoyable process.

Northern Comfort

Worst of Winter

Willi Miller pinned her best blouse to the rope line, shaking her bare hands to keep the blood moving, as she reached into the broken plastic basket for something else. She should have done this miserable chore before she went to work this morning, but she didn't have the time. Short and thin-boned like her mother, but yellow-haired like her father, Willi spun around for her boy, who stood a half-foot away, staring at the dog whimpering and jerking its chain. "There you are, Cody. Stay near me," she said.

Her boy, dressed in a one-piece red snowsuit, his mittens packed tightly on his hands, didn't say a word. He only made noises that sounded like words, and he was seven. His 'Ma,' Willi had decided, was exactly as an animal would say it.

Earlier this afternoon, she got Cody at the babysitter's house, where the van took him after school. Willi was a hairdresser at the Lucky Lady Beauty Shop in nearby Tyler although the running joke among the gals who worked there was it should be called the Unlucky Lady because of the stories the customers told about their men. Cheaters, drunks, and bums, the whole lot of them, it seemed, by their complaints.

The 'Lucky Lady' was busy today with high school girls who wanted their hair curled and piled high for the semi-formal tonight. They were fun customers, so excited about their dates and the big Friday night ahead, she didn't mind their lousy tips. Willi remembered not that long ago she did the same.

She fed Cody cereal after they got home just to hold him until she made dinner. He ate a few spoonfuls before he began playing with it, making a mess as usual, so she dressed him in his snowsuit and took him outside after she lowered the damper on the wood stove.

Now, Cody walked beneath the hanging laundry toward the dog, named Foxy by her grandfather, who used to own the brown, short-haired, pointy-eared mutt. Willi called to her boy, who moved step by step across the snow, breaking through its icy crust until he sank to the top of his boots. He turned toward his mother. His green eyes peered from beneath the brim of his cap. Yellow snot bubbled from one nostril.

"Yeah, I'm watchin' you," Willi said, bending for a towel.

Snow seeped through a crack in her right boot. Cold numbed her toes. She should put duct tape over the brown rubber, but it was her only pair, and it'd look like hell.

"Hey, Cody. Where're you goin'?"

Her boy marched with fast little feet past the junked truck to the back of their house, where his sled, a cheap thing she bought, was propped against the wall. "This is a red sled," she told Cody in the hardware store.

Her boy uttered a sound that might have been "red" but only she would know. She understood his ways most of the time. He wanted things tick-tock regular when he ate, what he wore.

Her eyes followed her boy, dragging his sled, grunting, toward her. He dropped it at her feet and sat inside. The heels of his boots kicked up and down. "Maaaaa," he called.

Willi sighed. Cody wouldn't let up until she gave him a ride. Her boy liked it when she towed him in his sled along the driveway to get the mail. He made happy chirps and flapped his mittens. She wiped her hands on her black jacket, a man's, too big and open in the front because the zipper was broken. Its bottom swayed against her legs as she walked.

"All right, Cody, but just a little ride."

She reached for the towrope and pulled Cody in a large circle. His mouth formed a wide, sloppy smile, and he let out gleeful sounds as Willi went slowly, then gained speed. Her feet sank through the snow, although the sled glided easily on its surface. She was careful to stay on the flat part of her land, away from the edge of its tabletop, where it plunged onto her

4

neighbor's property then to one of the town's main roads below. When she squinted, she could see the Mercy River flowing through its snowy valley like a blue vein on a woman's wrist.

Round and round Willi towed her son. She slipped on the packed ring of snow, and her straight, yellow hair dropped to her jaw when her knit cap fell. Cody's head rocked back as he yelped in pleasure. After a while, she stopped, out of breath.

"I gotta finish hanging the clothes before it gets dark. Alright?" she told Cody, although she did not expect his answer.

She picked her hat from the snow. The sun was low in the sky, and the dark smudge spreading from the west likely carried more snow. Willi frowned. It'd be too much trouble to take the clothes down again. She hated this part of winter, mid-January. It snowed every day, not much, but enough to keep the road crews going with their plows and sanders. Winter always has a week like this, unsettled weather, the worst of the season, of the year, as far as she was concerned. Often, it happened after the thaw, so that brief warm spell seemed like one cruel joke.

She bent for one of Cody's shirts. She had to work faster because the clothes were stiffening inside the basket. After she hung them, they would freeze into thin slabs, like shale, and after a day or two, they'd be dry. If she had any money, she'd buy a dryer. She glanced toward her house and saw missing clapboards. She'd fix those, too.

When she was a girl, she used to keep a mental list of what she'd get if she were rich: stuff like pink high heels and a long white coat. None of them seemed practical for a town like Hayward, where half the roads were dirt and fancy things were in other people's houses. Now, she'd buy a car that worked without worry and hire a lawyer to make her ex-husband, Junior, pay child support.

Her boy bucked his body while he lay on his belly inside the sled, wailing as if he were wounded. Willi shook her hands and grabbed a pair of jeans from the basket.

"Shit, I hate this life," she said.

You Did Good

Miles Potter was loading tools onto the bed of his pickup's cap when he noticed the sky in the west was as gray as a saw blade. He wore a thermal shirt beneath his red flannel, a Christmas present from his mother, and jeans ready to let go at the knees. He was tall and bony, so he put a lot of expression in his walk. His hair was dark and long enough to give him that young pioneer look popular with the men of Hayward, where he always lived, except for the couple of years when he tried college.

Miles had a few toolboxes to go, the wooden ones he built when he started working as a carpenter. Their handles were smooth and dark from the oil of his hands. His only boss, Linwood Staples, said it was the best finish that money couldn't buy. Linwood had something to say about any subject, especially the weather, one of the man's favorites. If Linwood were here with Miles, he'd take one look at the sky and say, "We better get home before that thing gets us."

The toolboxes were Linwood's idea. His first day on the job, Miles showed up with tools he carried in two compound buckets, stuff his father had in his garage. Linwood was doing Miles a favor. He came back in the spring from college with grades too poor to return and searching for something that might matter. He needed a job, and Linwood, then in his late sixties, needed help although he'd never admit it.

The first day, a decade before, Linwood's mouth chewed on his thoughts before he said them. "A customer can tell a lot about the carpenter he hires by what he uses to carry his tools." He pointed to the back of his truck. "I'm partial to metal boxes, but I keep them painted nice. You might want to

6

try something other than a couple of dirty, plastic buckets."

That night, Miles built the first toolbox, cutting the lumber with a handsaw. He used butt joints to form its sides, attached a dowel for its handle, and rubbed linseed oil into its surface. The next day, Linwood's lips formed a grin as he appraised the workmanship. "It's a start," he said. "At least I won't be ashamed to be seen with you. Just stow it in the back of my truck."

That was as close as Linwood ever got to a compliment. Miles worked with the man for five years before he retired, and then he was on his own.

Miles slid the last toolbox across the bed of his pickup and shut the cap's door. He returned to the house he was helping to build for a couple from New York, a getaway place for the weekends. Eventually, they'd retire here, they pledged, but Miles doubted they'd last. The New Yorkers who moved here couldn't understand why the general store closed at six or that they could only get three channels on their TV and no cable. It's 1982, for goodness' sake.

Miles asked himself how someone from the city could be happy living in a town with only one store, one bar, and one traffic light. Sometimes he barely stood it, and he was a native.

He found his canvas jacket on the living room floor near the window seat the woman wanted so badly. She planned to read here and take in the view, a remarkable picture of the Berkshires, Miles agreed. He spotted chimney smoke and a long church steeple rising through the trees like the point of an awl. He guessed it was a village in Tyler, a town west of Hayward. To the south, he saw flat, white packages that must be snow-covered fields in neighboring Conwell.

Miles crouched to examine the raised-panel front of poplar wood he made for the window seat's base. He stood, content he did this one well. His part of this job was winding down. The crew finishing the floors would take over, and then the painters. He'd be back to finish the trim for the contractor in a month.

He eased the truck down the steep driveway the owners had built so the house would have unobstructed views. Hc snorted.

Wait until they see how much it costs to keep it plowed, but then they easily could afford it.

The truck's rear end slid sideways. The small amount of wet snow from this morning had iced, so he put the pickup in four-wheel-drive when he reached the road. Snow was stacked high along State Route 133, and the winds blowing across the cornfields cut the banks in waves. Three wild turkeys clung to the branches of a tree, their bulky bodies bending the limbs to the snow's top.

He stopped at the Hayward General Store to fetch his mail from the attached post office, where he kept a box for the convenience. Today all he got were bills, which he stuffed into the pocket of his jacket. Inside the store, he pondered the selection of canned food, settling on soup, and then he ordered a pound of hamburger at the deli counter. He grabbed two six packs of beer for the weekend, although he thought he had some at home.

"Planning a big night, Miles?" the woman at the register asked.

They used to be neighbors when they were kids, so he knew she was being nosy-friendly in a small-town way. Miles remembered her as a silly girl who painted her fingernails bright pink and worked on her hair a lot, her best feature.

"Well, I thought after dinner and a couple of beers, I might pull the splinters outta my hands." He winked. "Want to join me?"

"Oh, go on," she said, blushing.

He figured to call Beth, the woman he had started seeing on a semi-regular basis last spring. Beth moved to Hayward a few years ago to teach at the elementary school. Theirs was a relationship without much fire, he admitted, but it contained a pleasantness that kept it rolling.

"Good night now," he said.

It started snowing again while he was inside the store, so Miles hit the wipers to clear the truck's windshield. He was a few miles from home when he slowed his truck in the winding section of State Route 133. To his right, the Mercy River's lively blue water chopped around snow-capped stones. To his left, a white hill dropped sharply from its ridge.

Miles stared.

Something red slid down its slope.

"What the?" he said.

The road took a turn, then another, and for several minutes, trees blocked Miles's line of sight. He was on the straightaway when a large, bright object shot between the trees and over the snowbank. He saw it clearly now, a child airborne on a sled but did not believe it. The sled hit the panel of his truck's door, and then there was another fuller thwack. The pickup slid sideways as Miles braked. Tools shifted across its bed.

"Oh, my God. Oh, my God."

Jumping from the cab, he scrambled to the child lying face up in the road. Miles's insides twisted hard as he knelt to listen for the boy's heart, but his chest was silent. His own beat in his ears. "Come on, little boy. Breathe for me."

Miles placed his lips against the boy's mouth, the flesh inside sugary and wet, as he tried to breathe life back inside him. He massaged the boy's heart, his movements short and determined.

From somewhere else, Miles heard the wail of a woman, and as she got closer, her wild gasps. "Cody," she yelled. "Cody!"

Miles did not look up. The voice belonged to Willi Miller, who lived high on the hill. This must be her son. His fingers pushed his chest over and over as he peered into his vacant, green eyes. Miles cradled the boy while he removed his jacket and folded it beneath his body, then brushed fresh snow from his brown, woolen hat. He breathed into his mouth.

"Don't stop, Miles. Don't," Willi cried as she crouched beside him. "Come on, Cody, wake up," she pleaded with her son. "You gotta wake up."

Miles continued, but there was no change in the boy. Vehicles stopped, including one of the town's plow trucks, and Willi ran toward it, her voice piercing, "Help, help! My boy's hurt!" Then she was back, telling Miles the truck driver called for help on his radio. He listened to Willi's voice as he pressed the boy's heart gently and blew air into his mouth.

He did not stop until two volunteer firefighters came beside him. One tugged him aside as the other got to work on the boy. "Let him take over, Miles," the firefighter said. "You did good."

Miles stepped back. How long had he tried to help the boy? He didn't know. A small crowd had formed on the snowy road, watching, and a town cop directed traffic. Finally, a boxy ambulance rolled between the rows of parked vehicles, its headlights casting beams across the snowy road. Miles closed his eyes. You did good, the firefighter said. Miles shuddered. How wrong could the man be? When he opened his eyes, Willi was beside him, wringing her hands, red from the cold. In the light, her tears looked iced.

"Willi?" he asked hoarsely, but she did not answer. "Willi."

It startled him when she pushed her face against his chest. She sobbed, and he pulled his arms around her. She shivered beneath them.

"Will he be okay?" she asked.

"I hope so," he whispered so close to her that he smelled wood smoke on her clothes. "I'm sorry."

"My baby," she moaned.

He held her tighter.

Now it came to Miles. Something was wrong with the boy. He saw him and Willi around town. He didn't know the diagnosis, but it appeared he was born that way. Cody was in Beth's first-grade class last year. She said he seemed normal, but he wasn't. When he grew up, he would have to live in a group home or stay with his mother as Willi's husband, Junior Miller, quit them years ago.

Willi held onto Miles, crying. A trooper stopped beside them. "Mrs. Miller?" Willi lifted her head from Miles's chest. "Would you like me to take you to the hospital?"

She wiped the back of her hand across her face. "Yes," she whispered.

The trooper studied Miles. "Are you the boy's father?"

"No," Miles answered in a low voice. "I was driving the truck."

"Stick around, sir," the trooper said.

The cop brought Willi to a cruiser as the rear doors of the

ambulance closed. She gave Miles a backward glance, and his finger jabbed the air to signal he would follow. Her mouth opened in a silent "oh," and then she was in the cruiser's front seat. The air filled with sirens.

Suddenly, he felt chilled in his red shirt and from the wet knees of his jeans. He found his jacket on the ground but did not wear it. He walked with his head down through the crowd. A man from town asked if Miles was all right, but he waved him away.

Miles found another trooper shining a flashlight on his truck. Someone must have turned off the engine since he couldn't remember doing it. Road salt coated the truck's black paint, so it was easy to see where the boy and his sled hit the driver's door. A dent was on the panel.

"Is this your truck, sir? I need to ask you some questions." The trooper was all business. "How about your license and registration?"

Miles removed his license from his wallet to hand it to the cop. He needed to get the truck's paperwork from the glovebox. But first, he gestured at the snowbank where the boy's sled launched toward his pickup. "See over there?" He shook his head. "It happened so fast, the way he hit the side on his sled. I never expected it. I tried to help. I really did." He eyed the stony-faced cop. "Will he make it?"

Miles covered his face when the cop said no. The impact broke the boy's neck. Little Cody Miller never had a chance.

Top Speed

Willi's ride was top speed as the state trooper kept pace with the ambulance. Snow fell hard, but she saw the ambulance's lights through its thick, white curtain. She tried to picture the paramedics inside working on Cody, trying to save her boy.

She felt herself tighten and her foot hit the floor when the cruiser took a sharp curve, but its tires hung tight as they made the turn.

"You all right, Mrs. Miller?" the trooper asked.

The cop was a big man with a crew cut that looked as if it had been painted on his scalp in tiny, black strokes.

"Yeah," she said faintly.

It was odd to be called Mrs. Miller. The only other time that happened was in the hospital when she had Cody. She supposed the trooper was saying it out of respect. Well, Miller was her last name even though she was no longer married to Junior.

"How old was your son, Mrs. Miller?" the trooper asked.

Willi felt another cry coming on, but she held her own. "Cody would've been eight on his next birthday June 9," she said. "He was in second grade, but he got special help in school because of the way he ...."

She stopped before she tripped over the ending.

The trooper nodded. "When did you notice your son was missing?"

She closed her eyes for a moment.

"I was hangin' somethin' on the line, and when I looked over, Cody was gone. I ran after him, but he was movin' too fast on his sled for me to catch him."

Willi saw her boy lying on his stomach, heading down the

12

icy hill on his sled as if he were molded to its plastic like a toy. She chased him, but she kept sinking into snow nearly to her knees, which slowed her descent as her boy's quickened. Her heart beat hard like chopping wood.

"I see," the trooper said.

"I hollered and hollered, so he'd roll off the sled. But...." Her words spun into a high, soggy whine. "When I got there, he was on the ground and Miles was tryin' to help him. I was hoping. But it looked bad, real bad."

The trooper's hum sounded low in his throat.

Gone

Willi sat on a couch in the hospital's waiting room, her face buried in her hands. A nurse was beside her. "Mrs. Miller, is there anything I can do for you?"

Willi didn't answer. She took the tissues the nurse gave her, although it wouldn't be enough to soak her tears. She glanced up when her sister, Lorna, rushed through the door. Ma came after.

Lorna was the first to speak. "What's this that cop said about Cody being in an accident? Where is he?"

"Cody's gone," Willi whispered. "My little boy is dead."

Lorna joined Willi in her sad chorus. Ma held a fist against her mouth.

"The doctor says Cody didn't suffer." Willi's breath broke in stabbing pieces. "He says he died right away."

The nurse stood and Lorna took the place beside Willi on the couch. She patted her sister's arm. "I'm so sorry, Willi. He was such a sweet little boy."

"Yeah, he was." Willi raised her chin. "I told the doctor I wanna see him again. I don't think I can do it alone. Could you come with me?"

Her mother held her purse close to her chest. She stayed a few feet from her daughters. "You sure that's a good idea, Willi?" she asked.

"Yeah, Ma, course she wants to. It's her boy." Lorna turned toward the nurse. "Can you fix it for my sister?"

The nurse nodded. "Stay here," she said. "I'll see what I can do."

Willi rested her head on her sister's shoulder, but she sat up when Miles Potter walked soft-footed into the room.

"Cody died," she sobbed.

His head quivered with little nods. "They told me. I'm so sorry."

Miles went down on one knee and clutched Willi's hand.

"It wasn't your fault," she said. "He just flew into your truck. I-I-I tried to c-c-catch him, but the snow was too deep. I really tried."

Ma and Lorna's hard eyes were aimed on her and Miles. She knew what they were thinking. What was he doing here? Miles must have seen it, too, because he dropped Willi's hand. "I should leave you all alone," he said. "Mrs. Miller. Lorna."

Willi shook her head, wanting Miles to stay, but he left anyway. The corners of Ma's eyes dug deeper toward her nose.

The nurse was back. "Mrs. Miller, you can see your son," she said.

Ma shook her head. "I'm gonna wait for you here."

"Ma," Willi said.

Lorna stood.

"Come on, Willi. I'll go with you to see Cody."

All Alone

Cody's body lay on a table. His red suit was off, so he was in the clothes he wore to school, his green striped shirt and corduroy pants. His hair, yellow and straight, hung flat against his head. Willi stopped, but Lorna grabbed the back of her arm, yanking her sister forward. The nurse stayed behind.

"Oh, Lorna, look at him," Willi said.

"I know. Poor, little boy." Her sister's voice was hoarse. "Come on. You can do this."

Willi studied her son's face. Cody didn't seem asleep on the table. Only empty. She bent to kiss his lips. "Oh, Cody, baby, I love you. I love you so much." Her fingers shook as she stroked his hair. "I really tried to catch you. I did. I'm s-s-sorry, Cody. I'm so sorry."

Willi kissed her son's face several times. She touched his shoulder.

"Come on, Willi," Lorna said. "We should go."

"I don't wanna leave him. He's all alone."

She cried so hard she felt as if she'd break apart.

"But, Willi honey, there's nothin' you can do. Cody's gone. I'm really sorry."

Willi nodded slowly. She gave the boy one last kiss before her sister led her from the room.

Not Coming Back

Lorna backed her car into Willi's driveway as far off the road as it could make it. Lorna had to leave at four the next morning for her job at the bakery in Tyler, and she might have to bully the car onto the road. Nearly a half-foot of snow had fallen since the afternoon, slick stuff when it packed because the temperature had risen a few degrees. They had been lucky to follow the plow truck after they dropped their mother at her house. Willi refused to go inside when she saw her stepfather's truck.

"Another time, Ma. Okay? I feel beat."

Ma had reached forward in the back seat to lightly stroke Willi's cheek. Her mother's fingers smelled like cigarettes. "I'm sorry about Cody. You did your best by him," she had said. "I'll call you tomorrow."

Now, the two sisters walked silently in the darkness, aiming their path toward the kitchen light. Their boots squeaked when they pressed into the snow. Willi's breath got louder as she worked up another cry, and her sister wordlessly handed her a wad of tissues she swiped from the hospital.

Willi slowed her steps. "I dunno if I can go inside."

"Yeah, you can." Lorna gave her arm a tug. "I'll be here with you."

The dog barked when they were several yards from the house. Willi walked toward the doghouse to unchain Foxy. The dog leaped and ran around while Willi moved toward the clothesline to get the laundry basket. She stood in a spot where light shined from a window in her house. She turned toward the blackened hill where Cody left her. Headlights slid as steadily as shooting stars on the road below.

The state trooper thought it odd, her hanging laundry in the cold, almost dusk, but she explained she had a washer, but no dryer. Didn't she know it was going to snow? No, she told him.

Willi lifted the basket and shuffled to the kitchen shed where she stored firewood and assorted junk. Lorna was already there, her arms filled with logs. The dog was at the door, waiting to be let inside.

"How about getting the door?" Lorna asked.

Willi dropped the snow-covered basket on the shed's ground floor and moved forward to open the door. The light in the kitchen came from two bare bulbs on the ceiling.

"Jesus, what a light," Lorna complained.

Willi didn't have the heart to say it used to have a shade, but Cody broke it last summer when he flung a hard, pink ball toward the ceiling. Both shouted, he in terror, she in anger, as shards of glass showered them. She pinned Cody, shrieking, on his bed while she worked to free a piece of glass stuck in one foot, hoping she got it all because he'd never tell her.

Now, Willi sat at Cody's seat at the table. The cereal he didn't finish was a yellowish mush. She bit her lip as she tapped his spoon on the table's wooden top. It was a sugar spoon, the kind with a fluted bowl, and a hand-me-down from her mother. Cody wouldn't eat without it. Willi remembered the time the spoon got lost, and she tore the kitchen apart until she found it beneath the refrigerator. Cody hollered with delight when he saw the spoon in her hand. He made no words but a happy bark. She expected no more.

"Here, I found it," she told him and herself.

Lorna blew on the live coals in the wood stove before she lay in pieces of kindling and three logs inside the firebox. The stove was the only source of heat for the house, once a hunting shack, until her grandfather winterized it and added the bathroom on the back. Every fall, Willi wrapped the house's bottom layer with tarpaper, the way Pa showed her, tacking it against the clapboards every few feet, before she set bales of hay around the perimeter. She looked forward to the first snow because it sealed the house from the cold.

Willi watched blankly as the fire caught behind the stove's glass door.

"Get out of your coat," her sister said.

18

Lorna took after Daddy's side of the family, the Merritts, tall and husky. Willi felt childlike when she stood beside her.

Slowly, she obeyed her younger sister, letting the black jacket fall against the back of her chair.

Lorna spoke softer, "Can I get you somethin'?"

Willi shook her head. "Just sit with me, Lorna."

The phone rang. Lorna jumped to get it.

"No, she can't, and don't call again." Lorna slammed the wall phone's receiver before she returned to Willi. "A reporter. Do you believe it? What an asshole."

The phone rang again. This time, they let the machine pick up. The minister of the Hayward Congregational Church said he was sorry about Cody. "I can help, Willi, with the arrangements," he said. "There's a funeral home that would do everything for free. Let me know."

Lorna stood to take the call, but Willi told her to let it be. "I'll do it tomorrow."

Lorna nodded, and after a long pause, she said, "Who's gonna tell Junior?"

Willi raised her fingertips to her lips. She shut her eyes. The trooper had asked about Cody's father. She told him she had lost touch.

"Do you want us to find him?" the trooper said.

She told him not to bother. His mother and father knew how to reach him.

Willi had heard from Lorna that Junior lived in New Hampshire with a woman, one in a series since he left her and Cody. She preferred that he lived out of state. He wasn't going to give her money no matter where he was. At least, she could go anywhere in town without having to see him.

Willi opened her eyes.

"Don't ask me. Lorna, I wouldn't call him even if I knew where he was." Her voice was shrill. "How can you forget he walked out on me and Cody? My boy was only two. You think it's been easy for us?"

"No one told you to marry Junior. Even Dad was against it. You wouldn't listen."

"Dad? Dad? Don't you mean Joe? He's Ma's husband, not

19

our father."

Willi slapped the tabletop so hard Cody's bowl and spoon clattered. Ma married Joe when Willi was twelve. She never thought the man who sat in his boxer shorts, drinking beer on the back porch, as much of a father figure. Lorna, who was five years younger, had more of a bond with him. She didn't remember much about their father, who died when she was younger than Cody. Joe had another family before he married Ma.

"All right, Joe then." Lorna dropped her voice. "But Junior's still Cody's father even if he wasn't much of one."

"You're right about that, and I don't wanna hear you stickin' up for that bastard."

Lorna sighed. "All right, all right. Just forget what I said."

After Junior became a deadbeat, her grandfather invited Willi and Cody to move in with him. She and Cody shared the bedroom that later became Cody's after Pa died. Willi, named for her grandmother, Wilhelmina, cooked and cleaned. She drove Pa in his pickup wherever he wanted to go.

"You're a fine girl, Willi," Pa told her every day.

Junior last saw his son two years ago. He came with a girlfriend a few days before Christmas. The boy shrieked and clung to her the whole time.

"He doesn't know you," she told Junior and his girlfriend, a brunette in jeans so tight their seams must have left marks on her flesh.

Now, Willi glared at her sister. "Sorry, Lorna. Somebody else will have to tell Junior."

"Okay, okay, forget about it. I know how to reach him if I have to."

Lorna got to her feet and yanked off Willi's hat. Her yellow hair crackled with static.

"What are you doin'?"

Lorna began to clear the table. "You just rest there."

Willi glanced around the room. Cody's toys and clothes were everywhere, but she couldn't bring herself to touch anything. The dog sniffed the floor, searching for her boy. Willi sighed. "No, Cody's not here. He's not comin' back. Come on, girl, I'll feed you."

Willi got up to get the bag of dried food from the counter and bent to fill the dog's bowl. With a sideways glance, she studied her sister, all business at the sink as she scrubbed and rinsed, her elbows moving like machinery. Willi admired her sister's energy.

"Here, give me Foxy's water dish and I'll fill it," Lorna said, and afterward, "All done. Time for a smoke."

Willi followed Lorna to the couch. She used to smoke but gave it up after the doctors said it was bad for Cody. She couldn't afford it anyway. She picked at the chapped skin of her lip as she thought.

"What kinda funeral should we have?" she asked Lorna.

"I dunno. Something small would be nice, but that won't happen."

"Why not?"

"You know how people are when somethin' bad happens. They may not have known Cody, but they do you." She jammed the butt in the ashtray. "Shit, it's almost eleven. I gotta get to sleep if I'm gonna be up in time tomorrow."

They had decided on the ride they would sleep together in Willi's double bed. The couch was too soft. Neither mentioned using Cody's.

"Why don't you take a shower while I bank the fire?" Lorna said. "I'll let the dog out for a coupla minutes."

"All right," Willi whispered before she went into the bathroom.

Willi stripped as she ran the water in the stall, so it'd be hot enough. Steam filled the small room, and in the mirror, her body, so thin her hipbones jutted like little wings, appeared to be moving in low-lying fog. She thought she heard Lorna talk on the phone, although she didn't hear it ring. Perhaps she called their mother. Or maybe she tried finding Junior. She touched the scar across her belly that she got when Cody was born. The doctor practically ripped him from her after his heart stopped.

She murmured when she saw his toothbrush next to hers.

"Willi Miller, you were a lousy mother," she said without any pity to her image in the glass.

That Tender Spot

Miles stopped at a bar he seldom frequented in Tyler on his way home from the hospital. He had a shot of scotch then began on beer, feeling the alcohol come on fast because he hadn't eaten since lunch. He sat at the bar, stripping the label from the bottle, not doing much of anything else, except scanning the rows of hard liquor and the fuzzy picture on the TV.

A man on the stool next to him tried to start a conversation.

"Sorry. I'm afraid I'm not much company tonight," Miles told him.

It was after eleven. Miles dreaded news about the accident would be broadcast on the TV, so he chugged the rest of his beer and drove home.

He used the phone in his kitchen. It was late, but he knew his parents were still up. Retired schoolteachers, they were snowbirds, living half the year in Florida. He didn't expect them back in Hayward until spring.

"What's wrong?" his mother said when she heard his voice.

He told her about the accident. "I just came from the hospital. Her little boy died."

"Oh, Miles, how awful. Let me get your father. He's watching a show."

He waited for his mother to push his father's wheelchair to the kitchen. His mother held the phone to his ear while Miles repeated the story. His father made a raspy gurgle when he finished. Then, his mother was back on the phone, talking in a wobbly voice that made her sound her age. She didn't have Miles until she was nearly forty. Dad was older. His parents didn't expect to have a baby after so many years. Our happy surprise, they called him.

22

"Miles, I wish we could be there with you, but we can't. It'd be too hard a trip for your father."

"Sure, Mom. Willi's little boy, Cody, did you ever have him in your class?"

"No, but I remember him. Such a fragile child." Her voice dropped. "Willi and all that business with Junior. Then, after he marries her, he leaves her and the boy. It hasn't been easy for Willi. I was surprised she had the patience, but I think she did the best she could. Don't you?"

"Aw, Mom, I just feel awful about all of this."

The only sounds on the other end of the line were fake laughter coming from his parents' television set. "What do you mean, Miles?"

"I mean, a little boy died after he slid into my truck. How should I feel?"

"Oh, dear, I wish we were there. Do you want us to come? It wouldn't be easy with your dad the way he is, but if you think we should."

"No, no, don't come. I'll call you in a couple of days. Bye."

Miles hung up the phone. Nothing his mother said had eased the pain. Mom never liked Willi anyway from the time she was a student in her third-grade class, complaining about her ragged home life, her poor grades, and her misdeeds. "That Willi," she used to say. Miles remembered Willi as the girl who had a hard time staying still. Once she dared the boys to climb onto the school's roof, and when no one would, she did it herself using the janitor's ladder.

His mother used to say when she looked at her students, she could see how they'd turn out as adults. She knew who'd be fixing her car and who'd be lending her the money to buy a new one. Sometimes her expectations erred. Certainly, it was true for her son. Here he was over thirty and unmarried. He worked as a carpenter.

Miles got another beer from the refrigerator and sat on the couch in an unlit portion of the living room. The flakes falling outside were large and featherlike. The storm was losing its strength.

The room had a large, paned window, one of the first things

23

he changed about this cottage to bring in more sunlight. It was a summer place when Hayward was a destination for rich people wanting to get out of the city. The walls were horsehair plaster on lathe, and the floors had wide pine planks. The first floor was open, except for the bedroom and bath. The second had space for two more bedrooms, but the only access was a folding wooden ladder, so it remained unused except for storage.

Miles rubbed his right temple, trying to ease the tension wound in that tender spot. He couldn't think of a worse day in his life. Nothing could touch it, not the rollover crash in his first car, the day he flunked out of college, or when his father had his first stroke. Until this accident, his life had been spared much trouble.

He couldn't lose the sight of the boy flying toward his truck or his still face as he tried to revive him. A few seconds either way, he wouldn't have been involved in his death although, as the trooper pointed out, high ledge was along that part of the road. A few yards and the boy would have hit stone.

"Stones and trees have no conscience," his former boss, Linwood, once told him when they drove to Fishers Hardware to get lumber. The store was set to close soon, and Miles pushed his pickup to beat the deadline. "Hit one, and it don't care. So, it might be a smart idea to slow this truck down a little. If we don't get those boards today, we'll get 'em tomorrow. I'd just like to be here for it."

Awakened from his urgency, Miles had felt foolish and enlightened. The store was closed, but one of the Fisher brothers, Homer, who was inside, let them conduct their business anyway.

Now, Miles guessed he could add a truck to the list of inanimate objects that have no conscience although he knew its driver did. He got another beer from the fridge. He should get the hamburger and the can of soup he left in the truck, but his boots were off, and he couldn't bear to go in the cold again.

The phone rang. His friend, Dave, was on the other end. "Jeez, I heard about the accident," he said. "How are you doing?"

"Not so hot," Miles told him.

Miles and Dave were long-time best friends. Dave's parents moved from Boston with a bunch of kids to Hayward when he was a boy. He so took to country living Miles joked he was a born-again redneck. Dave made a living through an assortment of jobs, all tied, unfortunately to the weather, which was a damn way to make a living. He maple-sugared in the spring, hayed in the summer, cut firewood, and at last resort, painted houses to support his wife, Ruth, and their two daughters. Miles sometimes helped his friend with sugaring, often his slowest time of the year.

"Is there something I can do for you? Want me to come over?" Dave asked.

"No, but I appreciate the call."

Miles drained the beer from the bottle and got up to get another.

Stuck

Willi awoke, fearful someone was moving inside her house, and then she realized it was Lorna getting ready to leave for the bakery. Her sister was in the bathroom.

"Lookin' for somethin', Lorna?"

"Yeah. Got any plugs? Never mind, I found some. You only got two left. Mind if I take one? I can't wait to go to the store. I'm bleeding like a stuck pig."

Willi saw red spots on the sheet where her sister slept. "Go ahead. Take 'em both. I can get more."

Lorna came to the doorway. A blue cardboard box was in her hand. "Go to sleep, Willi. I'll be back around two to help you."

Willi rolled toward the wall. Cold air squeezed through the cracks in the window frame, so she pulled the blankets around her. She closed her eyes, drifting off, but minutes later Lorna was back, touching her shoulder.

"Hey, get up, Willi. My car's stuck. I need you to give me a push. Hurry up. I'm gonna be late for work."

Willi threw off the covers. "Just let me get a jacket and my boots. There's some sand in a bucket in the shed."

Outside, Willi felt the peace that comes after a storm. The stars were as sharp as gems, and the moon was pared to a thin crescent, so close to being new. She held a shovel on her shoulder. Lorna carried the bucket of sand as they marched silently toward the idling car. The steps they made last night were half-filled with snow.

Lorna unlocked the trunk where she stored another shovel. She and Willi worked to clear the snow the highway truck's plow had pushed into the driveway. Lorna spread the sand where the car's tires would roll. "Ready?" she asked her sister, and Willi answered "yeah" before Lorna got into the driver's seat.

Their first try failed. Willi shoveled more sand beneath the tires, and then she gave the back of the car a long, strong push, so it pitched forward. She watched as the car's rear taillights moved down the road. Lorna honked the horn twice for Willi.

Willi walked back quickly to the house because of the cold and from habit. She never trusted Cody to be inside the house alone, even when he was asleep. The eyes of something wild glowed along the edge of the woods. She gripped the shovel and bucket until she was back inside her house.

It was about 4:30, by the clock, near her bed. Willi stayed awake listening to the noises of her house: the tired whirr of the refrigerator's motor, the creaks of the house's timbers, and the dog's steady snore. Normally, she'd hear Cody's wheeze in the bedroom next to hers. She always kept his bedroom door open, so the heat of the wood stove could make its way inside. She wanted to hear if he was having trouble breathing. His lungs were so weak he had pneumonia three times.

Willi heard a plow truck's rumble. Her neighbor's caretaker was here to clear the driveway. Nathan plowed but never charged her. She offered once to cut his and his wife's hair, but he said he was only being neighborly.

Cody liked watching the truck. He laughed and pointed at the window.

"Yeah, Nathan's truck," Willi would say, and Cody laughed.

The truck beeped as it backed. The blade's edge made a scraping noise when it hit the dip in the driveway. Willi rolled toward the wall and wondered if the man knew what had happened to her little boy.

Following Through

The next morning, Miles parked his pickup next to Willi's car. Another was in her driveway, which meant she had a visitor, an unexpected hitch. He hoped it wasn't her mother or sister. They made their feelings clear last night at the hospital. If that were the case, he'd make the best of it. He wasn't backing away.

He followed the path of crushed snow to the side shed. A dog began yapping in the yard, but its chain stopped it from reaching Miles. "Hey, there, it's okay," he said calmly, but the dog kept up its racket.

Miles knocked on the kitchen door. Willi's face was knotted and pale when she finally answered. She pulled at the strands of her hair.

"Miles."

"I came to see how you're doing, Willi."

"Not so good." Her voice thinned to a whisper. "Come in. The cold's getting inside the house. I've got company."

Her head made a quick tilt to the left. Miles knew the man at the kitchen table, the Rev. Jason Hood, pastor of the Hayward Congregational Church. Miles had spent little time there since he became an adult, outside of weddings, funerals, and a couple of repair jobs. But he recalled the Rev. Hood told good stories in his sermons. Sometimes he used people who lived in town to make his point, quite entertaining, but Miles didn't see a reason to attend church unless you believed in its religion. He no longer did.

"Hey, there, pastor," Miles called, and the man smiled over paperwork spread on the tabletop.

Pastor Hood walked toward Miles. He extended his hand. "Miles, how are you doing?"

28

He shook the minister's hand. "Lousy if you want to know the truth."

"I see."

The three of them stood near the door as an awkward silence slid over them.

Miles spoke finally. "Excuse me, pastor, but I have something private to tell Willi."

The minister gave an understanding sweep of his head and placed his hand on Miles's shoulder. "Son, if there's anything I can do, let me know."

Miles nodded, although he did not intend to ask. He doubted anyone, even this man of God, could ease his grief. The minister returned to his seat.

Willi waited until he spoke. She wore a man's woolen shirt that reached the knees of her jeans and hung past her shoulders.

"I want to pay for your son's funeral. It's the least I can do."

Willi squeezed her eyes tightly. She said 'oh' with such pain it sounded like the call of a bird. He sighed. Miles worked it out early this morning when he drove to the bank. He had no idea what a funeral would cost, but he'd gladly give her all he had. He withdrew a thousand from his savings account.

"Please, Willi, let me do this."

"You don't have to. The pastor's got a funeral home that'll do everything for free."

"Free," Miles repeated, raising his voice so the pastor turned their way. "How about the flowers? The church? I can pay for that."

"We're only having one arrangement, and Ma wants to do it. The church isn't gonna charge me." She gripped her hands. "We'll be fine. Really. Thanks anyway."

"The ambulance? Who's going to pay for that?"

Willi lowered her eyes. "The state pays for Cody's bills," she whispered.

Miles reached into his jacket pocket. He pressed a roll of bills into her hand, but she shook it away.

"This is for you."

"No, I-I-I don't need it. Really."

29

"Please, Willi, take it. Let me do something for you. I have more if you need it."

She raised her chin. "Come to his funeral. It's Monday afternoon at one. It'd mean a lot to me if you did."

Miles's hand curled around the bills. "I plan to go. If you need something, anything, call me first. Yes?"

Willi's fingers twisted over each other. Her green eyes shined with tears. "Yeah," she whispered.

Miles shut the door behind him. He checked back before he placed the bills on the doorstep, weighing them down with a clay flowerpot he found on the shed's dirt floor. Head bowed, he walked outside where Willi's mongrel dog barked and charged as far as the chain allowed.

"Take it easy," he told the dog. "I'm leaving."

The Arrangements

Willi sat at the kitchen table, her head bent slightly, as the Rev. Hood offered a prayer. They were finished with the funeral arrangements. It didn't take long, even with Miles's interruption. The service would be simple: some words by the pastor and the hymns she let him choose. He would arrange for a small obituary in the local paper. People would want to know.

Cody's body was cremated, so there wasn't any need for pallbearers. The Rev. Hood suggested having a photograph of her son, so people could remember how he looked. Willi thought the framed one she gave her mother for Christmas would do.

Rev. Hood stroked his chin. "What about his father?"

Willi shrugged. "His family's tryin' to reach him in New Hampshire." Her eyes dropped toward the paperwork on the tabletop. "I haven't heard from him in a while. We lost touch."

The minister gazed upward.

"Oh, Jesus, give this woman peace and keep her boy beside you in heaven," he prayed.

The Rev. Hood's voice floated so soft and high, he could have been singing in her kitchen. Willi welcomed his prayer, but her mind could not hold on to its words. She didn't know if there was a heaven, but if there were, she was sure her son was with Daddy and Pa, and they would watch after him.

"Her son, Cody, was an angel on this earth, so innocent, Our Lord, so loved by his mother."

In the beginning, she and Junior were grateful their son, whose middle name was Randall for Daddy, had survived his birth. He had come so close to dying inside her. But she saw as the months passed, Cody wasn't like other babies. He grew

31

slowly. He didn't do the things he should at his age. Something was wrong. Disappointment hollowed her insides like a sharp-edged spoon when the doctor explained why. Their son was brain damaged. Junior, who came with her to the office, yelled at the man. He threatened to sue the doctors. Of course, he didn't follow through. He never did with anything about their son.

"Lift our hearts, oh, Jesus, lift them high." Willi flinched when the minister's warm fingers covered her hand. "God bless you, Willi."

Willi didn't know what more to say, except thanks again. So, she felt relieved when the kitchen door flew open, and Lorna marched inside. Her sister held a wad of bills aloft. "Shit, Willi. Tell me what the hell's goin' on here? A thousand bucks on your step!" She stopped. "Oh, sorry, pastor."

"That's all right, Lorna. A thousand dollars. Well, well." The Rev. Hood smiled at Willi. "I believe it's time I went home. I need to make a few phone calls. I'll see you both Monday. Come a little early if you can."

Lorna lit a cigarette after the pastor left.

"I still haven't gotten a hold of Junior. You believe that? My boss said I could use the phone at the bakery. I called information, and he doesn't have a phone in his name. I don't know if he has a cell." She took a puff. "You happen to have the name of the woman he's livin' with in New Hampshire? I bet the phone's in her name. You know how Junior is."

Willi closed her eyes longer than a blink, as if she had hurt herself and was trying to deal with the pain. "Yeah, I do know how Junior is," she said.

"So, you don't."

"Really, Lorna, do you expect me to know who Junior's sleepin' with now?" Willi's voice was hoarse. "I stopped keeping in touch with him. Why bother? He didn't care about his son then. I bet he doesn't now."

"Shit, Willi, that's cold."

Willi stared at her sister. "Cold. Yeah, that's the way I feel. And I'm not apologizing for it."

Lorna stubbed the cigarette in the ashtray. "Okay, okay.

32

Maybe his brother Mike remembers the name of the bar Junior hangs out at," she said. "He went up there one time to see him last fall. Remember?"

"No. I don't care what Mike does either."

"Gee, Willi, you're impossible."

"Yup, that's me."

Willi reached for the brochures about urns. She chose a metal jar that looked as if it were made of silver, a tasteful choice, Pastor Hood had assured her.

Lorna threw the bills, all hundreds, on the table. Willi stared at the money. It was the most she had ever seen before.

"So, who left the money?"

Willi sighed. "It must've been Miles. He was here before you came." Willi watched the features on Lorna's face deepen. "He wanted to pay for Cody's funeral, but he doesn't have to. He tried to give me money, but I wouldn't take it."

Lorna leaned closer to Willi. "What! Are you fuckin' nuts? He could afford to give you a lot more than that. His family's loaded. Besides, I heard he was buying two six packs just before his truck hit Cody."

"You think he was drunk?" Willi said. "That's not the way it happened. Cody slid into the side of his truck, and Miles didn't drink. I would've smelled it on him."

Lorna shook a finger at her sister. "All I'm sayin' is what I heard at the store when I stopped for cigarettes."

Lorna's accusations wore on Willi. Everything did: the minister's visit, their questions about Junior, the money, the white flakes flying outside her windows. A state trooper came this morning to ask about the accident until finally he said, "I think I have enough, Mrs. Miller."

Willi got to her feet. She glanced at the money but didn't touch it. "I'm gonna lie down for a while."

Her sister's face softened. "Yeah, you do that. I'll take care of things."

In her room, Willi lay fully dressed beneath the blankets. She heard a light knock at the kitchen door, and then Lorna was talking with her neighbor, Nathan. Their voices carried easily through the thin wall of her bedroom. He had brought food his wife made. She wasn't surprised. They were good neighbors. On several occasions, they gave Willi a ride to work when her car broke down. She closed her eyes and saw Nathan holding her son on his lap as he drove the farm's tractor. Cody clapped his hands. His head rocked back against Nathan as he laughed.

"Martha and I are so sorry about what happened to Cody," Willi heard Nathan say. "How's Willi doing?"

"She's sleeping right now. Let me take that from you. Funeral's Monday at one by the way."

Willi rolled onto her side and watched the snow fall outside her window.

Low

A state trooper came to see Miles in the afternoon, and once again, he explained what he remembered about the accident. He was driving. The snow was falling. The boy, Cody, came down the hill and over the bank so fast he didn't have time to stop his truck. He tried his best to bring the boy back. The cop asked a few questions and didn't stay long.

Afterward Miles lay on his couch, the radio on low as he drank beer. He watched the snow fall until he had enough. He called Beth. "Hey, it's me," he told her. "Did you hear about the accident?"

"Yes, I did. I tried calling you a few times," Beth said. "Maybe you should get yourself an answering machine."

Miles was glad he didn't have one. Given the circumstances, people either had to talk to him in person or not at all. "Yeah, sometime," he said.

"Why don't you come over? I'll make dinner."

"I'd like that. Thanks, Beth."

Miles was still feeling a little lit from the beer by time he got to Beth's. She made a chicken dish he liked and opened a bottle of wine. They talked about what happened.

"You must feel so awful about this," she said.

"You bet I do." The lip of the wine glass rested against his mouth, so his words formed a hollow sound. "You bet I do."

Beth used the teacher's voice he grew up with, his mother's voice, kind but firm, always in charge. His grief eased a bit when Beth stood behind him and wrapped her arms around his shoulders. Her hair tickled his neck and cheek. He smiled.

"Thanks for trying to make me feel better."

He slid back the chair, pulling Beth onto his lap. He kissed her quickly with closed lips. She was a pretty woman, with light brown hair that must have been blond when she was a girl. She

35

wore lacy underwear whenever they got together. Her skin was soft and sweet smelling. So, he kissed her again.

Country People

Miles flushed the rubber down the toilet. He leaned naked over the running faucet of the bathroom sink, checking his face in the mirror. He looked like hell. His skin was puffy. His color was off.

He shut the water.

When he returned, Beth was lying in bed, smiling, and wearing a nightgown. He sat on the edge of the mattress as he slipped on his boxers. He leaned into the pillows.

"What was he like?" he asked when he finally spoke.

"You mean Cody? He was a handful, but he had a full-time aide when I had him in my class. He didn't talk much, so it was hard to know what he was learning. But he loved it when I read aloud, and he always wanted to sit on my lap or his aide's." She turned onto her side. "I think his mother tried hard with him. She was even learning the sign language we were teaching him." She paused. "You knew her a long time. Right?"

"Uh-huh. All our lives. Willi and I were in the same class. There were only ten of us. I lost track of her when she went to voke school. When I came back from college, I'd see her around with Junior."

Beth frowned. "But."

"But what?"

"Well, I never understood how she could marry her stepbrother."

The way Beth spoke she made it sound as if she were the only one in Hayward to know this bit of information, and now she was spilling her guts. The truth is everybody in town knew Willi's mother married Junior's father.

"So?"

"So? It's kind of weird, don't you think? Marrying your

37

stepbrother?"

He shrugged.

"Well, it's not like they were blood relatives. They didn't even grow up in the same house. Willi was maybe in sixth grade when her mom married Joe Miller. She and Junior didn't get together until years later. Eyebrows were raised, but only because Junior's a real jerk, and everyone but Willi seemed to see it at first. It was pretty rough on her when he split."

Miles tried to read Beth's expression.

"I suppose. Well, you know country people."

"What'd you mean by that? I'm one of those country people."

"No, you're not. You're not a redneck."

"Redneck? You're right about that. But those people work hard, and they stick up for the things they believe in. What do you think you're doing in Hayward anyway? Missionary work?"

Beth scowled as she picked at the shiny fabric of her nightgown. "That wasn't very nice. I don't think I'm better than those people."

"Yes, you do. That's all right. They probably think the same about you."

Miles gazed into her eyes, as blue as the cold water of the Mercy River. He raised his hands in surrender.

Junior

Junior Miller sat at the end of the bar of the Bull's Eye Tavern. He wore his brown hair long and a full mustache extended below his lower lip. This was his favorite seat because it gave him a clear view of the television set and his girlfriend, Sherrie, who tended bar. And, if he used the long mirror hanging over the bottles of hard stuff, he could watch who was coming and going behind him. He only had a couple of enemies in this New Hampshire town so far, but it's always smart to be sharp in a place like this.

"Hey, Sherrie, get me another Bud. And put it on my tab."

"Sure, honey."

Junior gave her a wink. He and Sherrie had lived together since summer in a single-wide trailer she owned on the edge of town. They met here at the Bull's Eye. It was the thing they had most in common. She worked there. He drank there. From his experience, he found any romance that started in a drinking establishment had a short life expectancy. This one was nearing its end. He saw the signs. She went to bed without brushing her teeth. She left her dirty underwear on the bathroom floor. Then, there were her digging comments. She didn't hold back anymore. Junior? He paid halves on everything. They had fun in bed. But he hadn't once felt the urge to tell Sherrie he loved her.

He nodded when a guy sat beside him, another regular. He was a carpenter, although this being the slow time of year, he was probably doing something else unless he was very good or lucky. Junior drove truck for a lumberyard, but only a couple of days a week. It was enough to keep him with money for beer, gas, and cigarettes until things picked up again.

"How's it goin'?" he asked Junior.

"It's still goin'."

Junior peeled the label from the bottle of Bud as he waited

for the next. Sherrie was busy with the bar's other customers. Saturday night. There was no better place to go around here. The town had a restaurant, Junior took Sherrie there for her birthday, but it was too fancy for his liking. It was for city folk whose idea of playing in the snow didn't involve machinery but two slats on their feet. The Bull's Eye was a bar for townies. Snowmobiles, pickups, and junks filled the parking lot. There was no live music tonight at the Bull's Eye, but somebody kept the jukebox going. Junior listened to the clack of pool balls and the clang of the pinball machines set off to the side. He might try his luck later.

Sherrie popped the caps off two beers. "Here you go, Junior." She nodded at the guy on the next stool. "Same?"

"You must've read my mind, sweetheart," he said.

The phone behind the bar rang. Sherrie went for it. Her back was to Junior, and she held one finger in her free ear. She turned toward him briefly. She yanked on the cord before she carried the phone to the bar top. "It's for you," she said. "It's some woman named Lorna. Says she's your sister."

Junior saw suspicion in Sherrie's eyes. "Yeah, she is, sort of. A stepsister. My pop married her mother. What does she want?"

"Wouldn't say. Told me she needs to talk with you. Says it's real important."

Sherrie handed Junior the receiver.

"Hey, Lorna, that really you?" he said into the phone. "How the hell are you?"

"Yeah, yeah, it's me all right. I finally tracked you down."

He strained to hear Lorna's voice over the noise. "Track me down. What for? Your sister put you up to this? This about money again?"

Lorna was silent. "No, it's not about money. It's about Cody. He was in an accident." She paused. "Cody died, Junior. Yesterday."

Junior held the phone tighter to his ear. "What'd you say? You gotta speak up. It's so damn loud in this bar."

"Your boy died in an accident yesterday."

"What'd you say, Lorna? I still can't hear you."

Junior felt a heavy hand on his back. One of the guys from

40

the lumberyard tried to get his attention. The man grinned beneath his beard.

He heard Lorna say, "Junior, you listening to me?"

Junior put his hand over the receiver. "Hey, buddy, not now. I'm on this call." He was back on the phone. "Start over."

Now, Lorna was practically yelling into the receiver. "Cody. Cody's dead."

His voice matched hers. "What do you mean Cody's dead? What the hell happened?"

Sherrie and the guys around him stared. He didn't care.

"He was on a sled," Lorna said. "He got away from Willi and he slid down that hill behind her house and at the bottom he crashed into a truck." Another pause. "The doctor said he died right away. He didn't suffer."

Junior gripped the phone. The news slammed him like that guy's hand. He closed his eyes. "Lorna, tell me. Who was driving the truck?"

"Miles. Miles Potter."

"That asshole didn't do somethin' to keep outta my boy's way?"

"The cops say it wasn't his fault."

Junior tried to swallow. "Not his fault?"

"That's what they said."

"Sure."

"You gonna come to his funeral? It's Monday. The whole town's gonna be there."

"Funeral."

Junior's heart revved like the engine of his snowmobile. He listened to Lorna talk about the funeral plans. "You don't have to worry about money 'cause the funeral home's doin' everything for free," she said. "The pastor helped work that out. The old ladies at the church are taking care of the food for the reception afterward."

He heard half the words Lorna said.

"How she doin'?"

"How do you think Willi's doin'? She's taking it really hard. I'm staying with her."

Junior tried to remember the last time he saw Willi and their

41

boy. Maybe it was around Christmas after the old man died. She made it clear she wanted nothing to do with him. Neither did the boy. It got real easy to forget he ever knew them.

"Okay."

"You gonna come to the funeral or not?" Her voice had a sharp edge.

"When is it?"

"I told you Monday. In the afternoon."

"I gotta tell my boss. I'll call Pop." He glanced up at Sherrie. She was pouring beer into a pitcher for a waitress. "Lorna, I need to ask you somethin'."

"What?"

"How old was Cody?"

"You dunno? Shit, Junior, he was seven."

"That's what I thought."

"Hey, I gotta go. Willi's getting outta the shower."

"Uh-huh, thanks for telling me."

Junior dropped the receiver onto the phone. He took a swig of beer. Then, he stared at nothing.

Sherrie stood in front of him. "You okay? You get bad news or somethin'? Is it one of your parents?"

He shook his head. "Yeah, I got bad news alright. My little boy died. Lorna said it was an accident."

Sherrie's mouth dropped. "You never told me you had a kid."

He shrugged.

"I guess I didn't."

"That's a pretty big secret to keep from someone you live with. Don't you think?"

He shrugged again.

"I haven't seen him in a while. He lived with his mother back home."

"How old?"

"Seven. He wasn't born right. The doctors said he had brain damage. But she did her best with him, you know, his mother."

"What's his name?"

Junior sighed.

"Cody."

Black Dress

The next afternoon, Ma barged into Willi's house with a grocery bag in her arms.

"There you are," she said.

Ma came alone yesterday to check on Willi, staying about an hour. Today, Joe was with her. Willi, who sat on the couch, drew up her legs, and wrapped her arms tightly around her knees. She didn't say hello to Joe.

Ma pulled black fabric from the paper bag and shook it out. "I found the dress. It was in the attic, like I said. What do you think?"

The dress was loose like a sack, an old style, and the fabric faded nearly gray. But Willi decided it was good enough. She would wear the cameo her grandfather gave her one Christmas. The brooch belonged to his wife, the nicest thing she owned. It might make the dress look better.

"That's fine, Ma," she said. "Thanks."

"Here, I'll just put it on your bed."

Willi didn't say a word to Joe after her mother left. She didn't look his way.

"Is that coffee I smell?" her mother said when she returned.

"Yeah, Lorna just made some. She went to the store and should be back soon. You wanna cup?"

"Sure. How about you, Joe?" Ma asked.

Her stepfather grunted.

Joe had the recliner, her grandfather's favorite spot, and where he died one afternoon while he took a nap. Cody kept tugging at the man's long, thin fingers, shouting "Pa, Pa," but Willi, who had been making dinner, knew he was gone when she went to check on him. Her grandfather had been on a slow decline for a while. She kissed his forehead and patted his thick, white hair, such a kind man to love his granddaughter and great-grandson so. He took them in, but he never made Willi feel like they were a bother.

Pa's funeral drew so many, people had to stand in the vestry of the Hayward Congregational Church. His brother, Boyd, and some of their pals picked and sang the songs they shared with her grandfather. He planned it all out a year before he died.

"Now, I don't wanna make this funeral too sad," Pa had said, as he dictated his instructions to Willi one night. "When my buddies play 'You Are My Sunshine,' remember that one's just for you and Cody."

She cried when he said it. "Don't leave us, Pa," she told him.

"Ah, we all have to go sometimes," he said. "And you and Cody have made my last years some of the best. Bless you two."

She grieved hard when Pa died two springs ago. He lived a long life, although one marred by the early deaths of his wife and son, her father. He used to say music was his closest companion until she and Cody moved in with him. Of course, Cody's funeral would be sad. How else would it be for a little boy?

Willi eyed Joe, who was stretched out in Pa's recliner. His gut bulged like the backside of a hog beneath his flannel shirt and over the buckle of his belt. His heavy beard was a couple of days old. Willi sighed and stood to get the coffee. She filled the mugs at the coffeemaker, fixing them with milk and sugar the way her mother and stepfather liked.

"Here you go."

Willi set the mugs on the low table in front of the couch and recliner, then returned to her place on the couch. Her mother sat beside her. "Thanks, Willi," her mother said, as she handed a mug to Joe.

Her stepfather sucked at the coffee's top layer. "I hear my boy's comin' to the funeral," he said.

Her mother gave Joe an encouraging nod. "It'll be nice having Junior there. Don't you think, Willi?"

44

"I'm sure not holdin' my breath for that," Willi said sharply.

Joe gave her a beady-eyes glare, but she didn't care. No one was going to tell her how she should feel about Junior. Willi raised her head taller.

"That's a shitty thing to say," Joe said. "He's the boy's father."

"His name is Cody."

"Yeah, Cody."

"And if you wanna know the truth, Junior was a real lousy father." Willi's voice began to lift. "He didn't see Cody or pay for him. He didn't care at all, and that's the truth."

Her mother nervously cleared her throat. "Willi, I can tell you're upset about your little boy," she said. "Still, it'll be nice if Junior comes."

Willi shook her head.

"No, it won't."

Joe's boots made a loud thump when he swung the recliner's footrest back in place. He nodded toward his wife. "Marjorie, let's hit the road," he growled.

"I haven't drunk my coffee."

"Leave it."

Willi didn't say a word. She watched Joe go first, and then her mother, who turned at the door. "I wish sometimes you'd try a little harder to be nice to Joe," she said.

"Bye, Ma," was all Willi told her.

Linwood

Miles slept late and drank again until he ran out of beer. He wished he had more, but stores couldn't sell it on Sundays, an old law. He smoked some homegrown pot he got from his buddy, Dave, though it was too weak to do him any good. His mother called, but he had nothing new to offer.

When the phone rang afterward, he almost let it go, but when he picked it up, Linwood's voice was on the other end of the line. "Son, I heard about your trouble." Linwood's voice was so dry it could have been made of kindling. "They were talking about it at the store this morning."

"It's a mess."

"The death of a child, especially a boy like Willi's, can cut the legs off anyone."

Miles swallowed. "I went to see her. I told her I'd pay for his funeral, but she said I didn't have to. The funeral home was doing it for free."

"Yes, they'll do that when a child dies and if the family is poor," Linwood said.

"I left her money anyway."

"That's good, Miles. But maybe there's something else you can do for that girl. It's been a hard life for Willi so far, her father dying so young, and then her mother marrying Joe. I know Joe and Marjorie. I bet they haven't been much help to her. No doubt you'll find a way."

"Thanks for calling, Linwood."

"I'm afraid I haven't said much to ease your pain. I can tell. Why don't you come see me? I don't get around so easily anymore. My joints. "

"I'll do that, Linwood."

When the phone rang minutes later, Miles didn't answer it.

He watched TV, and although no show interested him, he stayed with it until early the next morning.

At Church

The next day, Miles used a needle to dig at a splinter stuck in his thumb. He sat on a stool at the kitchen counter, carving through the calloused skin with the needle's point. The splinter must have been in there a while, probably since Friday, the last day he worked, because it was building puss beneath the surface.

"Holy Christ."

Miles checked the clock on the kitchen stove. He had to leave for Cody Miller's funeral now or he'd be late. He dropped the needle on the counter. He'd just have to bear the small pain. It certainly didn't compare to the ache in his stomach. Last night, he slept badly with the same jarring nightmare: Willi's boy lay motionless on the snowy road. No matter what Miles did, he couldn't help the boy.

"Let's get this over with," he told himself.

When Miles reached the Hayward Congregational Church, he parked his pickup in front of the elementary school next door, far from any other vehicles. He walked head down past the white, wooden building where he and Willi went to school and where his mother taught until she retired. Miles dug his hands into the pockets of his coat and kept going toward the church's front door. Again, the sky dumped snow. A town sand truck drove past, its strobe lights flashing yellow like torches, its hopper spreading sand and salt in arced lines across the whitened road.

Inside the church, people filled the pews from the center aisle outward. Miles went left, past a church deacon, choosing a place to sit midway, the place his family sat every Sunday when he was a boy. Members of the Potter family were on the committee when this church was built over one hundred fifty years ago. Ezra, Nathaniel, and Zachary Potter's names were inscribed on the plaque hanging on the wall to the right of the pulpit. Tall, stained glass windows lined the side walls, their wooden trim painted a nice off-white by his friend Dave. He had hired Miles because it was such a big job painting the ceiling and walls, which required staging and drop cloths to protect the pews' red velvet cushions. They got the job done in less than a week three winters ago, pleasing the pastor who didn't want the Sunday service disrupted.

A choir loft was behind the church's low pulpit, and an organ with pipes rose up the wall. The organist played something subdued, although Miles couldn't feel its effect. He exhaled deeply. His mother called this morning to see if he was going to the funeral. Yes, he told her, because Willi asked him. But he would have gone even if she hadn't.

There was no coffin, Miles was thankful, but a large floral piece and a silvery jar, which he supposed contained the boy's ashes, arranged on a table with a framed portrait of Cody. The photograph, one of those school pictures with a grainy, blue background, was large enough, so Miles could see the boy's face was animated, not like the boy he tried to save.

Miles knew almost everyone in church: folks from town and members of Willi's extended family. Many were dressed as if they came here from their work, wearing flannel and denim. Their heavy jackets hung open. He had worked alongside many of them. His eyes shifted to the right end of his pew. His neighbors, the Buells, tipped their heads. Old man Buell, who smelled faintly of cow manure, wore a brown canvas jacket over his overalls. Miles felt overdressed in his navy blue suit and long wool coat.

He recognized a group from the elementary school two rows over. Beth was with another teacher. Their eyes locked briefly, but she turned away. He didn't care about her either.

In a pew ahead, Miles saw Junior Miller's mother, Grace. She wore a yellow plaid coat, and a hat of gray, fake fur, which looked like a mound of dead squirrels atop her head. The woman glanced around the church, her head jerking in such sharp movements she resembled a bird of prey pecking at its quarry. Miles knew there were hard feelings still over the divorce, although it happened years ago. But he thought at least for this occasion the family could have been more welcoming to Grace. She's the boy's grandmother after all.

A few people pointed his way and whispered. He didn't need to know how they felt. He worked at the splinter with a fingernail until he spotted Willi and her sister, Lorna walk in tandem down the center aisle. Willi was a head shorter than Lorna. In her loose black dress, she appeared breakable. Their mother, Marjorie, and her husband, Joe, came behind them. They were a sour couple, the type of people who responded to a friendly greeting about good weather with the rejoinder, "Yeah, but it won't last long." Grace Miller gave the four of them the eye as they took their rightful places in the church's front pew. There was no sign of Junior.

His Innocence

Willi glanced up when she heard voices. Lorna whispered for her to slide over, and then she discovered it was for Junior, who arrived as the organist pressed the hymn's final chords. Willi stared at her ex-husband, feeling too wooden to do anything.

Junior looked like an outlaw with his long hair, leather coat, and the cowboy hat he clutched in his hands. He swallowed so hard the ball in his throat rose up and down. The ligaments in his neck grew as taut as cables.

"Come on, Willi. He's waiting," Lorna hissed.

Willi knew everyone in church was watching, so she moved closer to her mother. Lorna shoved over to give Junior her spot. To her right, Joe grunted, "Junior." Willi leaned forward slightly to check on her ex-husband. He gave a courteous nod and said her name in a low, rocky rumble. She leaned back as the Rev. Jason Hood began talking about Cody.

"I remember one time at the church fair when little Cody Miller got on the merry-go-round and just wouldn't get off," the pastor said. "He sat on the white horse, making happy little sounds as the ride spun in circles for hours. His loving mother stood on the side, watching him all the time."

Willi moaned as she remembered. The man running the ride wouldn't take her money.

"This sweet little boy flew down that hill like the angel he is now in heaven." The pastor turned toward Willi. "How could he not be? He was so innocent, so loved."

A woman from the choir sang "Amazing Grace," the only song Willi requested because Pa played it at so many funerals in town. Lorna hissed directions for her to stand or sit.

Mercifully, the service was brief, and then Lorna was telling

Willi to come with her down the aisle. Junior stepped aside to let them go. Willi swore his eyes were wet, but she didn't linger long on her ex-husband. Instead, she saw the other peoples' somber faces and bowed her head. Junior's boot heels thudded behind her.

Pastor Hood guided Willi, Lorna, and her mother to a spot in front of the vestry's stained glass window, so people could greet them. Joe was at the food table, helping himself to cake. That was okay by Willi. She didn't want him around. He wasn't part of her family. The most the man had said about Cody was, "Too bad about the boy."

The pastor stretched his hand toward Junior for a shake before he steered him toward Willi. She fingered the cameo pinned to her dress. "Right, here, Junior. Here's a place for you," Pastor Hood said.

Junior stood stiffly beside her.

"Willi, I'm sorry about what happened to Cody," he said in a low growl.

"Oh, Junior. It was awful."

His face softened as he reached for her shoulder, but his hand fell instead. He shook his head. "I should've come sooner."

Willi pressed her lips. She stared at Junior. Their bonds now were a failed marriage and the dead child he had abandoned. They had good times before that, she thought, but she didn't remember any of them. She wanted to tell Junior he shouldn't have turned his back on them. He shouldn't have been so cheap with his son.

"Yeah, you should've," was all she could say.

People grasped Willi's hand or patted her shoulder, telling her how sad they were about her son's death. Cody's babysitter, a woman her son adored, tearfully went on about what he meant to her. Willi knew she was being sincere. So many times, she found Cody asleep on the woman's lap. His head rested against one of her large breasts as he breathed hard through his mouth. She'd say in a soothing voice, "I think he had a tough day today," and Willi would be grateful for her caring ways.

"I'll miss that little guy so much," the babysitter said.

Willi teared up when the woman hugged her. "I know you will. You were so good to Cody. Thanks so much for coming." Willi then pointed toward Junior. "This is Cody's father."

"Mr. Miller, I don't believe we've met. I took care of your son after school," the woman said before she moved Junior's way.

For Willi, who had never felt such offerings of sympathy from the town, 'thanks for coming' became the best reply. Thanks for coming to the principal, who placed a thick envelope in her hand. Thanks to the man who worked at the sawmill with her father and grandfather, and who said Cody had her eyes. Thanks to her ex-sister-in-law, Mike's first wife, who showed up, and thanks to her cousins who drove in the snow from Penfield. Thanks to the teachers at the elementary school who had Cody in their class.

From the corner of her eye, Willi watched Junior labor with his greetings. Most knew him, of course, but for those who didn't, like the teachers at the school, he had to explain himself. "Yeah, it's a shame. He was a good boy," she heard him tell one teacher.

Junior didn't look any of them in the eye. He fingered his cowboy hat as he leaned toward her. "Willi, I gotta go outside for a smoke," he whispered. "I'll be right back."

His eyes had the nervous flicker of a man in trouble.

Willi knew he wouldn't return. "Thanks for coming," she told Junior.

She turned toward the waiting mourners.

Her neighbors Nathan and Martha were next. Martha gave her a quick hug. "Let us know if you need anything," she said.

Willi sniffed as her eyes began to fill with tears. She used her fingertips to wipe them away. "You've been thoughtful neighbors," she said. "Cody loved to see you drive your tractor, Nathan. Thanks for coming. Really."

The girls from the Lucky Lady Beauty Shop were together.

Theresa, the owner, kissed Willi on the cheek. "Oh, honey, we feel so awful about your little boy," she said. "Come back when you can. Alright?"

Theresa was the one who listened to her stories about Cody, like the time he fell asleep in a closet and she nearly had a heart attack trying to find him. Or how he came into her bed at night when he got too cold. Theresa called him 'Tiger' when he made his happy growling noises.

"Thanks for coming."

Willi turned when she heard a familiar voice. It belonged to her ex-mother-in-law, Grace Miller. "Sorry about your boy." Her smoker's wheeze squeezed her words. "I was glad to see my Junior made it to his funeral."

"I didn't expect it. I haven't heard from him in a long time."

Grace searched the vestry. "Where'd my son go? He was just here."

"He left to go smoke. He said he's comin' back, but I doubt it."

Willi studied this woman who last saw her grandson when he was four. Once she sent him a Christmas gift, an orange plastic car, so cheap it had no windows and the doors didn't open. Cody carried it everywhere until he finally found something else to love.

"I can see you're hurtin', Willi." Grace buttoned her coat. "I just wanted to pay my respects."

"Thanks for coming."

Grace gave a bounce of her head, and then she moved aside for the next person.

The line went on. Junior, as she predicted, did not return. Finally, she reached the end. She glanced around. Miles stood beside the vestry's tall wooden doors. She nodded. He stepped slowly toward her, his eyes so mournful she gave him a meek smile.

"How are you doing, Willi?" he said in a voice only she could hear.

"It's so hard."

She rested her head lightly against his chest, her cheek touching his starched white shirt. His arms spread around her, and they stayed that way until Miles whispered, "I should go."

"Okay, Miles."

He slipped slowly from her. She stared at the floor rather

than see him go. Then, her head was up. She forgot to mention the money. She took a step forward, but Lorna was at her side. She handed Willi a brownie.

"Here, take this. Eat it." She nodded at the shutting door. "What in the hell you doin' with him?"

Willi didn't answer. The ladies were clearing the plates and cups, so she went to thank them. "It means a lot to me," she told them.

The old ladies clucked and insisted she bring the leftovers home. They were good-hearted women. Every Christmas one of them dropped off a food basket wrapped nicely in cellophane and a toy for Cody. When Pa died, they all made food just like they did for Cody.

Lorna was again at her elbow. She was dressed for outside. "Joe wants to hit the road. He says the storm's getting real bad. He says it's gonna be tough getting up your hill. We could stay at Ma's tonight instead."

For Willi, staying at her mother's house wasn't an option. She'd tell Joe to stop at the bottom of the hill and she'd walk home in the snow.

"No, I need to get home. I gotta take care of Foxy."

Willi grabbed her black jacket from the coat rack and went toward the church's pulpit. Her sister followed, pulling off her scarf to wrap around Cody's photo. Willi took the jar. She rubbed her hands over its smooth surface, glad she had Cody's body cremated. She couldn't have stood to see a small coffin. Besides, the ground was frozen, so the burial could not have taken place at Hayward's Center Cemetery until the spring when the ground thawed. She hated thinking her boy's body would be in storage so long. But here, she was, holding a jar containing all of him.

"Ma wants the flowers," Lorna said.

Willi frowned. "You take 'em."

Lorna lifted the arrangement. She and Willi followed the center aisle's red carpet. "Have you thought of what you'll do with his ashes?"

Willi shook her head and tightened her grip on the urn. "No," she said. "I think I'll just hold on to 'em for now."

Too Much

Junior sat in his pickup with the engine running in the Town Hall parking lot across the road from the church. The wipers slapped the snow off the windshield. The defroster was on high. He lit another cigarette.

He smoked the first on the stone steps of the church but crossed the road when people began to leave. He didn't feel like talking about his son with any of them. That's why he went outside.

Junior hadn't thought of Willi and the boy for a long while. She had given up chasing him for money. It was easy to forget he ever knew them, except for those sentimental holidays when families are supposed to be together. He spent most of them with a woman or in a bar, where he called his parents to wish them a happy whatever and make half-hearted promises to visit soon.

Junior felt low when Lorna told him the news about Cody. But its full depth did not hit him until he showed up for his son's funeral. Sitting in the pew, he concentrated on Cody's photo. His son looked a lot like him at that age, except he had Willi's fair hair. Junior felt something heavy stove in his chest as the minister talked about the boy and Willi cried. He wanted to cry, too, but he couldn't.

Afterward, the minister insisted he stand next to Willi. His ex-wife was all skin and bones, but she managed to reach inside to thank everyone who stopped. They all loved her. He felt their accusing eyes.

Junior left the idling pickup when he recognized Pop leaning against the fender of his wife's car. Snow collected on the shoulders of his old man's jacket as he smoked a butt. He grinned when he recognized Junior.

"How's it goin', Pop?"

"Shit, this is one long, lousy winter, eh? Fuck. And it's only January." His father tilted his head toward the church. "That thing in there was somethin' else. Didn't know so many people cared about the kid."

"Yeah, it was. Miles Potter had a nerve to show his face." His jaw felt tight when he talked. "I never had much use for that fucker. I can't believe the cops are letting him get away with it. If it was me or you, they would've nailed our sorry asses."

Joe spat in the snow. "You're right about that, son."

"How's she holdin' up?"

Joe flicked his butt. The lit end sparked when it hit the snow on the church's driveway. "Willi? Lorna's staying with her. That little girl is tougher than she seems." He spit again. "I'm proud you came today."

Junior turned his head, so his father couldn't see his face. "I'd better head out now."

"Shit, in this weather? Why don't you bunk with us?"

"Nah, it's okay. I'm stayin' with Mom. I'll see you soon."

In the cab of his truck, Junior watched Willi grasp the metal handrail of the church's stone steps. She moved like a deer on ice as she cradled the jar in her arms. Lorna and their mother were right behind.

All he wanted was a boy to play ball and do the things normal kids do. He wanted a wife who loved him first. He gripped the steering wheel and rattled it hard. That wasn't asking too much, was it?

I'm Home

Miles stopped at his parents' house rather than go straight home. Now they only lived here for less than half the year. Miles paid to keep the driveway plowed and the walkways cleared as if his parents were coming home. He used the kitchen door. The heat was on low, just enough to keep the pipes from freezing. He went from room to room, flicking lights on and off, in the bedrooms and bathrooms, the library.

"Hello, I'm home," he said aloud.

He came to the living room, where he eyed the bookcase. The photo album he wanted was on the bottom shelf. He brought it to the couch, turning the pages to see his progress from his parents' precious baby to a boy. He stopped at the photo of his first-grade class. There were ten kids in that class. He stood in the top row. Willi was in the bottom and to his right. She pulled at the hem of her dress as if she was about to curtsy. She had a crooked smile.

"Oh, Willi," was all he said.

No Better Than Us

Lorna parked her beat-up Ford near the general store. Willi had stayed home since the funeral five days ago, and now she didn't want to leave the car. Her clunker didn't start, the battery drained from sitting so long in the cold. Lorna volunteered to take her.

Her sister made puffing noises as she leaned inside the car. "Willi, there's nothin' to eat in your house. You can't just live on the stuff I bring you from the bakery. Come on, get your butt out here."

Willi peered up at her sister. "I think it's time you went back home, Lorna. I can manage now. Really."

"Yeah, yeah, sure. It's 'cause of what I said last night about packin' up Cody's things. How I said it was too depressing to see all of his stuff all over the house. I'm sorry I said it and the other stuff, too."

Willi winced.

"I know he's gone, Lorna. I just can't do it now." She blinked back tears. "Please, Lorna. I just wanna be left alone."

Lorna gave her sister a square, hard look. "I was getting tired of that lumpy bed of yours anyways. And you snore." She paused. "Now get your ass in the store. We're here already."

"Okay, okay. I'm comin'."

Willi reached into her jacket pocket for a white handkerchief to wipe her eyes. She opened the car door and slowly followed her sister inside.

The store was filled with customers. Some stopped to offer their condolences, but a few stayed away, suspicion playing on their faces.

Lorna saw it, too.

She spun toward a woman, wife to one of the town's

selectmen. "Did you say somethin'? No? Could've sworn you did. My mistake."

Willi was embarrassed and grateful when the woman went to another aisle. She stood in front of the shelves of canned foods, trying to decide what soup to buy. It was too hard. Lorna dumped one of each kind in her handbasket until Willi got tearful.

"Please, Lorna, that's enough, please."

Lorna took the basket from her sister's hand. "Shush, I'm only tryin' to help. Let's get some milk and cold cuts. Do you need food for that mutt of yours?"

Willi couldn't keep up with Lorna. The woman had ticked off her sister, and now she was walking and talking fast. Then Lorna was out the door, with three grocery bags in her arms. Willi ran from the store to get to the car before her sister.

"That snotty bitch. Who does she think she is?" Lorna muttered as she dropped the bags on the back seat. "You should see how she is when she comes into the bakery. Talking about that precious son of hers. The *architect*." Lorna sneered. "She's no better than us. Don't you ever forget it."

"Oh, Lorna."

Watch Out for Joe

Back home, Joe's truck was in the driveway, its front end facing her dead car. The hood of his pickup was propped open. Ma waved to them. Willi had asked her mother if Joe could jump-start her car's battery. She was going back to work at the Lucky Lady on Monday and needed to get her car on the road.

Willi walked toward them. Her mother held off lighting her cigarette until she got a peck on the cheek. When Willi said hello to Joe, he rolled his lips as if he tasted something awful. "Your mother says you got some car trouble."

He reached inside the truck's cab for his jumper cables.

Willi's head was down.

"Yeah," she said.

Lorna went inside to put away the groceries. Willi shivered with her coat open while Joe attached the cables between his truck and her car. She eyed the bug shield on the front of his pickup that said, 'Watch Out for Joe.' She frowned.

Her feet shifted, partly because of the crack in her boot, mostly because she wished she had asked Nathan or a stranger off the road to help her. Everything Joe did was louder and rougher than it had to be, like the way he shut the pickup's door and flung open the hood of her car. His boots scraped the driveway's crusted snow.

"See those tires." He pointed. "The tread's shot to shit."

Willi kept silent.

Ma hooked up with Joe at the Pine Tree Tavern, the only bar in town, and part of her social life after Daddy died. Ma played Bingo on Mondays and Thursdays at the American Legion in Tyler. She went to the Pine Tree on Fridays and Saturdays, where she and Joe, in the process of getting a divorce from Grace, hung out.

Willi and Lorna met Joe when he came from the bathroom one morning. He wore a t-shirt and boxer shorts with its fly gaping open, so Willi got a glimpse of his hairy flesh. She turned away, grabbing her sister's hand to join her. Their mother came behind them.

"Put some pants on Joe, for goodness sakes," Ma said, laughing as he ducked behind the bedroom door.

Joe's overnight visits became a regular thing until he married her mother, and the house became his, too. They held their wedding reception, a pig roast, at the Rod and Gun Club. It's where she met Junior and his two brothers. Junior was Joe's oldest, then in his twenties. Mike was already married, and Dustin, just out of high school, had plans to go into the service although he never did.

The party was a raucous gathering to celebrate the old newlyweds with the adults getting drunk on free beer while a local band played Country and Western music badly. The men built a bonfire using pallets and pine logs that grew so large the neighbors called the fire department. Joe invited the firefighters to join the fun after they returned the engine to the station. All night Willi and Lorna stayed close to their cousins as they listened to the men swap dirty jokes and make loud barking laughter.

Now, Willi stamped her feet in the snow, wishing Lorna was beside her. The smoke from her mother's cigarette passed in front of her face. Ma gave darting looks at Willi, then Joe, who sat in the driver's seat, with one foot on the ground as he cursed and wrestled with the car's rattling ignition.

Willi relaxed when the engine caught. "Let 'er run for a while," he said.

"Thanks, Joe."

Joe disconnected the cables and bunched them in a roll. "Next time, missy, don't let a car with an old battery sit in the cold. And do somethin' about those tires before you get yourself killed. Then, I'd have to listen to your poor mother bitch and moan about you."

Willi studied the man's footprints on the dirty snow. She shook her head. Daddy wouldn't have talked that way to her.

Thin and Tired

Miles raised his finger to the bartender for another round before he slid off his stool. He walked between the tables of the Pine Tree Tavern, his home away from home these days, toward the door where nobody was standing. He dumped change into the payphone on the wall. Willi's voice was thin and tired on the other end of the line when she finally answered.

"It's Miles. How are you?"

"Miles."

She was silent. Miles huddled protectively over the phone.

"I was calling to see how you're doing."

Her breath stuttered.

He clutched the receiver tighter.

"It was a week ago," she finally said.

"Yes, it was."

Willi said Miles's name again, and then nothing as her cry turned reedy. He raked his hair with his free hand. Cold air washed over him each time the door beside him opened.

"Do you want me to come over?"

"No, my sister's here. I have to go." She worked at each word. "Thank you."

Miles hung up the phone and went back to his seat. He drank the shot fast, chased it with beer, and raised his finger for another.

Lucky Lady

Willi walked the icy parking lot behind the Lucky Lady, which joined Wayne's Variety Store on one side and the Chuck Wagon Café on the other. Red paint peeled off the building's clapboards. Wayne, the man who owned this skimpy strip of commerce in the middle of Tyler, said he was going to cover it with vinyl siding. 'Vinyl is final,' he liked to say, but that was two years ago, and he had done nothing since. Theresa, the woman who owned the Lucky Lady, didn't remind him because she figured it'd be an excuse for him to raise her rent.

"Wayne should just move his fat ass and paint this place right this summer," she told the girls in the Lucky Lady.

Everyone snickered.

Willi stopped in the entryway of the beauty shop. The light from the fluorescent fixtures buzzed and bounced over the large, pink room. Theresa hung framed photos of smiling, beautifully coiffed women on the wall above the row of hooded hair dryers. Their heads tilted on long, white necks, so regal, like hostesses in a banquet hall. The workstations were on the opposite wall. Willi's was neater than when she left it. Someone, likely Theresa, put pink carnations in a vase.

Alice, the other woman who worked here, wasn't in yet. Theresa was in the far corner washing a customer's hair at the sink. She gave a little wave with a soapy hand. "Hey, honey, gee, you're awfully early. Your first cut isn't until nine."

Willi glanced at the wall clock above the photo of the dark-haired hostess in white. It was 8:35. She smiled at Theresa until she remembered why. She didn't have to get Cody to school or to the babysitter's house if this was summer. She made hurried steps to the backroom to put away her jacket.

Theresa followed. "It's really great to have you back,

sweetie. Work will help."

Willi used the cuff of her turtleneck to wipe away the tears.

"That's what I hear." She paused. "Thanks for the flowers."

Her nine o'clock, a wash and cut, was five minutes late. The customer was a friend of her mother, a complainer who yakked about the lousy weather and the progress of her hairdo her entire time in the chair. "Make the top higher, will you?"

"Sure," she told her.

Willi teased the underside of the woman's gray hair. She made a satisfied grunt when she saw herself in the mirror and tipped Willi a buck.

"Sorry about what happened to your boy. Comin' down the hill and crashing into a truck like that. Poor little fella."

Willi thanked the woman as she helped her with her coat. "I'll tell Ma I saw you."

Willi got a close look of herself in the mirror. She twirled away, startled at how thin she had gotten living on coffee, soup, and toast. She swallowed hard and pushed the dollar into the front pocket of her jeans.

She did two more cuts and a color before she went next door for coffee. She gave her order at the counter to the waitress, a redhead overdue to get her roots touched up.

"It's nice to see you, honey. Chuck and I want you to know how sorry we are," she said.

Willi's head bounced in quick little jerks. She asked for two coffees, one black, for Theresa, one with milk and two sugars, for her. The griddle behind the counter smoked as the cook used a spatula to scrape charred bits off the surface. It was between breakfast and lunch, so the place was nearly empty. A man at the counter chewed with teeth that were yellow and broken. His head jiggled to the jukebox, a tune by Johnny Cash, one of Daddy's favorites.

In the far corner, another man sat at a booth, drinking from a mug as he read a newspaper spread in front of him. His back was to her, but Willi recognized Junior. She stepped to the left, so he wouldn't see her if he turned. The waitress handed her two sealed cups of coffee.

"We don't want your money today." She wiggled the

fingers of one hand. "It's on the house."

Willi thanked the redhead, but in her rush, nearly upset one of the cups. She gave Junior another peek. He had pulled his hair into a ponytail hanging down the back of his neck like the thick tail of a dog. His head and shoulders shook as he laughed at something he read. He was supposed to be back to wherever he lived in New Hampshire.

When Junior officially left her, he had been gone for days before he returned to their apartment for his things. He walked between their bedroom and the living room, shoving clothes into two duffel bags. Junior didn't talk except to make little stabbing comments. Willi sat on the couch with her arms wrapped tightly around her. Cody was asleep in the other room. Junior didn't even bother seeing his son.

"Keep the rest of the junk," he told her.

Junior put so much weight in his walk, his boot heels sounded like hammers over the linoleum. A woman waited in his pickup truck. Willi saw her through the window. She didn't say a word or cried until Junior slammed the door.

Now, Willi rushed toward the café's door and back to the shop before he noticed her.

Icy Drops

Willi was washing dishes when the rain began. She had let the mess pile up since Lorna went back home, and she was working on the pans with a rusted pad of steel wool when the icy drops hit the window like a spray of birdshot. She groaned. Rain in winter meant ice, and she only had a little sand left in the shed. She needed to go to the town's highway yard to get more. She would have to spread wood ash on the driveway tomorrow morning, so she could get to work. Ash didn't work as well as sand, but it might give the car's tires enough traction.

She thought about what her stepfather said about the tread on her car's tires. Maybe she'd use some of the money Miles left to buy four used ones. Lorna was being such a pest about the amount, complaining what he left was a cheap payoff.

"He should've given you a lot more. He killed your boy," Lorna said the last time.

"You're listening to Ma too much," Willi told her.

"Yeah, well, I hear he's at the Pine Tree every night."

"So what? I told you already. He wasn't drunk. The cops said it, too."

Willi had more than the thousand Miles gave her, in all nearly two thousand in cash. People kept handing her envelopes of money at the funeral. Maybe they thought she needed it to pay for Cody's funeral, but she had other wants, like a pair of boots that didn't leak.

She waited in the shed as the mutt, Foxy, darted into the darkness to do her business. The rain froze when it hit the snow, coating it with a clear, hard finish. Willi admired the shine until she heard scratching near the woodpile. Something large and dark rushed across the ground. A rat, she was sure.

Sometimes they traveled from the doctor's barns next door. Willi beat her feet against the ground to scare the animal, and then she used two fingers to whistle for the dog.

"Stay close, Foxy," she said, when the mutt bounded back.

Last year, a rat got through a hole under the kitchen sink, where she used to keep Foxy's food in a plastic pail. Willi hated the rat's dry, urgent sound as it moved inside the cabinet. Worse, she was scared it might hurt Cody. She got the trap from the shed, and remembering what Pa told her, she poured boiling water over it to get rid of her smell and used rubber gloves to place the baited trap beneath the sink. She heard the trap's snap while she lay in bed. In the morning, she carried the bloody mess across the road to the doctor's woods where she dumped the body. Afterward, she used a license plate from Pa's old truck to seal the rat hole. She hadn't seen one since.

Back inside, Willi stood in the center of the living room. Cody's toys were still in the spots he dropped them, except what Lorna had touched. Ma said she could store his things in her attic, but Willi wondered how much they would total. She planned to keep some of his toys and his schoolwork, the drawings that resembled tangled wires, sad souvenirs her son was not like other children. The rest she'd give to the Salvation Army. Who else would want them, except people poorer than her?

As she did every night since Lorna left, Willi went into the boy's darkened room to lie on his bed, smelling the oil from his hair on the pillowcase and the faint odor of pee from his bedclothes. She stared at the jar containing his ashes on his dresser top then closed her eyes. Tears pooled beneath their lids.

Willi replayed the accident. Moments before it happened she was not his loving mother, but a woman weary of it all, not thinking ahead. How long did it take to happen? Certainly enough time for her son's sled to slide beyond her reach.

Outside, the rain made a shirring noise as the wind blew its pellets against the house. She felt as if the ice covered her, each layer sealing her in sadness.

She used to sleep in this bed with Cody when Pa was alive.

She didn't mind the tight squeeze because she felt safe for the first time since her Daddy died. Willi kept the house clean and drove Pa on Sundays to his brother Boyd's house, so the two could play music and spin yarns. Boyd played the fiddle and Pa, the guitar. Together they plucked tunes they used to sing as boys like "Hobo Bill's Last Ride" and "My Blue-Eyed Jane." Some they made up.

"Take your time," Pa said whenever she did a chore. "I ain't in a rush no more."

Pa told her stories about what Hayward was like when he was young, how he used to work in a sawmill, retiring remarkably with all of his fingers. He described the large trees the loggers brought in and the interesting patterns he saw on their bark.

"I hated to cut those giants," he told her.

She liked to hear stories about her father, what he was like as a boy. He was the only child because Pa's wife had diabetes. "She spoiled him. It made him too tender." Pa's eyes went glassy and sad, and then he brightened. "But, my, he sure loved you girls."

The phone rang. Willi opened her eyes, but she didn't rise. She heard her voice on the machine, then a man's, a little high and coming from the back of his throat. Junior always breathed from the upper part of his chest.

"Willi, it's me, Junior. Pick up the phone. You gotta be there. This weather's so shitty."

Junior paused.

She stayed still.

"I'm visiting my mother for a while. I wanna see you." Another pause. "I'm sorry I ducked out at the funeral. It was just too much." His voice fell. "I really wanna see you, so call me at her house when you hear this. I think you got the number. Bye now."

After Joe married Ma, sometimes Junior or his brothers stopped by the house to visit their father. She and Lorna spied on the brothers as they drank beer with Joe or worked on their trucks in the garage. It wasn't until she was out of high school a few years he started paying attention to her. The first time was at the one-pitch softball tournament held each May at the Rod and Gun Club. Willi sat on a bench near the edge of the trees with her girlfriends. She held a beer can in one hand and swatted black flies with the other.

Junior walked with his teammates toward the dugout. "Hey, there, Willi, honey, you old enough to drink that beer?"

His buddy made a low remark. Junior cocked his head back. He had a big woman-pleasing grin.

Her friends kidded her about having such a handsome stepbrother. She told them to shut up. Junior was at least ten years older. He was a man with lots of women friends. Then Junior gave her a wink that made her smile.

Willi rolled in Cody's bed to face the window. Icy drops stuck to its panes.

"I hate you, Junior."

She said it softly, as if her boy were asleep beside her. She said it again, this time, louder.

Sticking

Junior rubbed his chin. *Where could Willi be? She was never a confident driver, so she couldn't be out in this storm. Maybe she stayed the night at her mother's.*

"Ah, shit, she's probably there listenin' to me make an ass of myself."

He opened the refrigerator for another beer. He popped the can and gulped.

"Hey, don't drink all my beer," his mother yelled from the living room.

"Don't worry, Mom. I'll get you some more tomorrow."

"You'd better."

Mom watched one of her shows. She liked the comedies and the women's movies, stuff that didn't interest Junior. He came from New Hampshire to replace the hardware on a few of her doors and to fix the leaking tap in the kitchen. It appeared little had been done around here since his old man split. The night he stayed after Cody's funeral, Mom complained her boys do nothing to help her.

"Aw, Mom. Don't feel that way," he told her.

But his mother was right about this anyway. Junior rarely drove from New Hampshire to see her. Both of his brothers used to live in Hayward until Dustin moved to Florida. Dustin and Mike had a big fight after they both got high and one brother said something stupid to the other. Mike took such a hard blow to his head with the leg of a chair, Dustin was sure he had killed him. The EMTs wouldn't go inside the house until the cops arrived. Nothing was done, boys will be boys and all that, except Dustin moved to Florida and Mike's hard head survived the blow. Mike still lived in Hayward with his second wife and their boys.

71

"Feel right at home. Lots of rednecks down here," Dustin wrote Junior on a postcard with an alligator on the front.

Junior took his beer into the living room. Mom sat on the sofa, her back squeezed against an electric heating pad. She worked in the mailroom of a newspaper, hand-stuffing circulars. She complained that lifting the bundles of paper was murder on her back. Mom used to be pretty when she was young, dark-haired with high cheekbones and full lips. Pop must have been nuts about her, but she let herself go when she had her boys.

Mom cackled when one of the show's actors told a joke. Her cat, a neutered tom, was tucked next to her hip.

"Sit down, Junior," she said, without taking her eyes from the set.

Mom's gallery was on one wall in the living room. All the pictures of Pop were long gone, but she kept the photos of Junior and his brothers when they were little. He stared at his own.

Mom must have noticed because she commented, "Yeah, I thought he looked a lot like you."

The boy's death kept sticking to him. He was a rotten father to Cody. No way he could make it up to the boy now. Willi was another thing. He shook his head, remembering what a hard time she gave him when he first started chasing her. He offered her a ride home from a softball game when her boyfriend, who played left field on his team, failed to show. Willi was asking around for a lift when he came up to her.

"I'll give you a ride home," he told her.

Willi gave him a wary smile.

"Sure I can trust you, Junior?"

He raised his hand and then crossed his fingers.

"Yeah, I promise I won't touch you."

The rides became a regular thing, and then one time he asked her to the barbecue joint in Jarvis. He told all his best jokes. On the way back, Junior asked if she wanted to go to his place, but Willi said sweetly, "Well, Junior, you're gonna have to be in love with me to do that."

He sighed. It took months to get what he wanted.

72

His mother set the ashtray she balanced on her thigh onto the coffee table. She got to her feet, yanking the cord of her heating pad from the socket. Her flowered housecoat slid over her body. "I gotta get to bed, son. Can you get the TV?"

"Sure, Ma. Hey, I was thinkin' of stickin' around for a couple of days. Things are real slow at the lumberyard. How d'you feel about that?"

"Shoot yourself."

She whistled for the cat and then shuffled in her slippers past Junior.

What He Owes

Miles heard the phone's ring tunnel through his brain. His head was heavy from drinking and unfinished sleep, but the caller didn't give up. He stumbled toward the kitchen and mumbled hello into the mouthpiece.

"Don't tell me I woke you, Miles," Linwood said over the phone. "My clock says it's noon."

"Yeah, I had a late night."

"Well, I need your help today. I got a project I can't do myself. My arthritis…. How about coming over? I'll make some coffee."

Miles rubbed his hair with the palm of his hand. It was Friday, which should be his last workday of the week, but it might be his first.

"I can be there in an hour. Is that all right?" he said.

"That'll be fine. I'll be waiting for you."

The step from his warm cottage stunned Miles. The temperature was in the teens, a snot-sticking cold that descended from northern Canada after the storm. Ice clung to the branches as if they were candied. The sky froze blue behind them.

Miles eased the truck from his driveway, then down the hill past the entrance to his neighbors' farm. Old man Buell used his tractor to tow a honey wagon filled with cow manure. Miles tooted his horn at Buell, and the man, wearing padded coveralls and an orange knit hat, waved with a gloved hand. A stream of white cloud shot from his mouth.

The Buells were the kind of neighbors who minded their own business but lent a hand when it counted. After Dad had his stroke, Mrs. Buell brought supper to his mother's house. Miles was happy to return the favor when he saw Buell and his sons replacing the farmhouse's roof. He went home for his tool belt, and then joined them on the roof, hauling bundles of shingles up a ladder and joking together. The sun baked his shirtless back that day, but he felt good when he went to bed.

Linwood took a while to answer the kitchen door. He was so stooped, the front of his plaid wool shirt hung loosely over the belt holding his chinos.

"Hey, Linwood. Glad you called."

Miles carried two boxes filled with hand tools across the linoleum floor.

"Come in, Miles, come in. Excellent timing." Linwood gestured toward the kitchen table. "You can just set those tool boxes down on the floor. I should've told you not to bring 'em. Want some coffee?"

Miles knew it would be useless to refuse, so he said yes. Linwood fixed the coffee with a little milk and so hot it would burn his mouth if he didn't drink it right. The man moved around the kitchen in a crooked little dance until he finally set two mugs on the kitchen table's red Formica top.

Linwood let his body fall onto his chair. "Here you go."

Miles tried not to make a face when he sipped the bitter brew. Linwood never measured when he put coffee grounds in the maker.

"That bad, eh? I guess I'm used to it."

"It's still better than what I made today. Where's Mary?"

"She's out with her sister, which is why I called you today. See, it's Mary's birthday soon, and I wanna give her a bunch of bluebird houses to put in the backyard."

"You want me to build birdhouses?"

"Uh-huh. I can't do it myself."

Linwood moved his fingers, which had gotten so gnarled they grew slanted from the joints of his hands. The copper bracelet he wore beneath the cuff of his shirt left a green ring around the skin of his wrist.

Miles leaned backward, amused, as Linwood explained the lumber he used would have to be weathered. They needed to trick the birds into thinking the boxes were rotted trees or fence posts, which was their preferred home.

"None of those fancy dovetail joints you like to make. Use

75

low-grade wood. I'm well aware it's not your usual high level of workmanship, but do you think you can do it?"

Miles grinned. "I think I can manage."

Linwood showed Miles a photo Mary found in a magazine. The boxes were long and vertical, and Miles supposed to a bird they might seem like a place to roost. Linwood planned to put them up in the spring as soon as he or somebody else could drive posts into the ground.

"It'd bring Mary great pleasure to have those birds flying around the backyard. She's been after me for years about the boxes, but you know how it is." Linwood smiled. "Five should do. I'll pay you well for your time."

Miles wanted to do this favor for Linwood. The man was a generous friend, although he, too, seemed puzzled by Miles's choice of profession. "Using your body's a tough way to make a living," Linwood would tell him. "You'd be better off doing something with your mind."

But Miles found he had a knack for fitting things together. Working with wood felt right in his hands.

He knew, too, he could move somewhere else, but he liked living in a town where he was on a first-name basis with most everyone, even if he didn't get along with some. He liked being in the woods and beneath stars he could see. He liked sitting in this old man's kitchen talking about bluebirds.

"I think I have some planks in my shop that should do the trick," Miles said. 'When do you want them?"

"How about in a week?"

"Sure enough. I have nothing else on my plate these days."

Linwood pressed his thin lips tightly as he studied Miles. He lifted his mug, took a drink, and set it down in a leisurely motion. Miles knew the man was moving onto something else.

"So, tell me, Miles. How are you making out since the accident?"

Miles cast his eyes toward the tabletop. "It's been kinda rough. I see it so clearly if I think about it. I can't even drive by the spot anymore."

"I see."

"After the funeral was over, I sat in the pew until everyone left to meet Willi." Miles shook his head. "I don't know how she did it. She kept saying thank you to everyone as Junior stood next to her."

"Junior was there?"

"Yeah, but he didn't stick around."

Linwood scratched the back of his neck. "You remember Willi's grandpa, Pete Merritt, don't you? The man had a gift for music, a real gift."

"Sure."

"Pete and his brother, Boyd, could pick all the old songs, stuff you don't hear on the radio anymore," Linwood said. "They played together at the local country fair, at parties, and a few old-timer shows at Town Hall. Pete's son, Randall, Willi's Daddy, sometimes joined them.

"Pete was a real gentleman. Must have been, to take in Willi and her boy after Junior left. She took care of him when he was near the end, and he rewarded her by giving her that little house. I really don't think she expected it. That's what I like about Willi. She's a little girl with a big heart." Linwood's eyes squinted, so they were nearly shut. "She must be going through a real hard time losing her boy."

"I gave her some money to help," Miles said.

"Yes, I remember you said that."

"I went to the funeral."

"I'm glad you did. But maybe there's something you can help her with."

Miles remembered seeing Willi drive her grandfather in his truck. Her little boy sat on his lap or beside him. Pete's face constantly carried a proud grin. Willi parked the truck next to the store's front porch and then ran around the side with a wooden crate to make a step for the old man. She stood there as he gripped her shoulder to ensure a safer dismount. Then, Willi pulled her boy onto her hip, and the three of them headed together for the front door.

He watched Linwood stroke his chin. That's the way it was with this man. He'd offer an idea and let him work out the rest.

Miles set his mug on the tabletop. "Yup, she took real good care of them," he said.

Blood Was Thicker

Junior went to see Pop in the afternoon, but instead he found Lorna sitting on the living room couch, counting and wrapping coins in paper. She had the TV on, a woman's talk show, while she fished through the pile spread on the coffee table in front of her. She had more change in gallon jars on the floor beside her foot.

"Hey, stranger, what brings you here?" Lorna asked.

Junior threw his winter jacket on a chair. "I came to see Pop. I'm on my way north."

"Dad should be here any time. He probably stopped at the store on the way home. He was low on beer."

Junior made note that Lorna always called his father, her stepfather, Dad, but Willi never did. He was always Joe or "your father." From what he remembered, Willi went out of her way to avoid him. She wouldn't say why, and Pop explained it away. "She's a nutty one, that wife of yours. Don't believe anythin' she tells you about me," his father told him.

Junior watched as Lorna picked through the pile for quarters. If you put her and Willi beside each other, you couldn't tell they were sisters. Lorna was one of those women who could be called big-boned, but she had a roundness beyond that. She had pulled her thick, dark hair back with a plastic band, and the tails of her blue flannel shirt hung over her jeans. Junior never saw her wear anything else. She couldn't be called beautiful. She had a bold, bossy way about her. But she could make some guy happy.

"Where'd you get all that money?"

Lorna kept rolling. "They're from the tip jar at the bakery counter. I'm putting it all in the bank 'cause I wanna buy a house someday. I'm savin' for the down payment."

She drew two cigarettes from the pack in her shirt pocket. He put the one she offered behind his ear.

"That much?"

She gave him a big grin.

"I'm gettin' there. Not everybody gets a house given to them." Her eyes bore through him. "Forget what I just said. It's okay Willi got the house. No one else wanted to take care of Pa. I sure didn't. Seems to me she earned it."

The smoke from Lorna's cigarette drifted toward his face. "So, how's your sister doin'?"

"Willi won't talk, but she's taking it pretty hard. She goes to work and then mopes alone at home." She took a puff. "His stuff's still all over the house."

"Did she tell you I called?" He frowned. "Well, I did, five times, and she didn't pick up the phone."

"Come on, Junior. Do you really expect her to? You saw what she was like in church. She hates your guts. And I don't blame her." She wrapped the quarters neatly in a roll. "Here's the story. My sister ain't gonna talk to you until you pay that money you owe her. And then, maybe, just maybe, she will."

Junior didn't speak for a while. He and Lorna always got along, but she was tighter with her sister. It was the same with him and his brothers. At times, they acted like enemies, but none would ever betray each other to an outsider. Blood was thicker. That's how it went.

"She wants money, eh?"

"Where you been, Junior? In some hole? You were a shit to my sister and your boy, plain and simple."

"Oh, yeah, I just heard you bitch about her gettin' the house."

"I told you, I didn't mean that. Besides, this is different. Men are supposed to take care of their kids. Sometimes I came over to give her a hand, watch Cody, sometimes Ma, but we were the only ones, except for Pa, of course. You're a real little shit, Junior."

She poked the lit end into the ashtray.

Junior felt his insides burn. He was ready to say something to put Lorna down, but Pop came home. He was opening the

79

refrigerator door and yelling for Junior.

Pop stood in the doorway. He tossed Junior a can of Bud. "Here you go, son. You still at that?" he asked Lorna, who gave him a big smile.

Junior held the can in his hand but didn't open it. "I'll take this for the road, if you don't mind. I've gotta get back to New Hampshire."

Pop leaned against the doorjamb. He lifted the front of his shirt to scratch his belly. "Hear of anybody lookin' for work for a coupla months? One of the drivers is out. His hernia busted. For Christ's sake, the dumb bastard drove himself to the emergency room," Joe said before he took a drink from the can and belched.

"Guy's out, huh?" Junior made a hum from the back of his throat. "It shouldn't be too hard to find somebody this time of year."

The Buy

Willi parked her car next to a display of roof shingles poking through a snowbank outside Fisher Brothers Hardware in Penfield. The store never seemed to change, not since she was a little girl coming here with Daddy to get new works for the toilet or something else to repair their house. She sidestepped the displays of stovepipes and paint cans, the floorboards bending and squeaking beneath her feet. The last time she was here was in the fall when she bought tarpaper to wrap her house and the red sled for Cody. Today, she had two things to buy: a light shade to replace the one her boy broke and a pair of boots, if they were still on sale, as one of her customers told her.

Horace Fisher stood behind the counter, one of three brothers, who were all in their seventies and too stubborn to let the next generation take over. He smiled at Willi. Horace had an extra-long space between his thin upper lip and the bottom of his nose, a common trait among all the Fishers, who lived in Penfield even before it was officially a town centuries ago.

"Willi, it's been a while. How are you doing today?"

They made small talk about her errands and the winter as he directed her to the lighting section, where she pondered for several minutes on the selection of glass shades. Horace showed her an opaque shade, a white rectangle with slanted sides. But she had her eye on a round one, its surface engraved like lace, which was twice as much. A few weeks ago, she would have taken Horace's suggestion, but now she didn't.

"That's a nice shade, but I like this one better. Now, I'd like to buy some boots."

She walked behind Horace, who carried the glass shade to that part of the store. The boots stood in lines on long, wooden shelves. Willi saw a pair of insulated ones from Canada, which cost more than she expected, but they appeared the warmest. She fingered the wool felt lining, thinking of the cold wrapping around her toes whenever she stepped outside.

Horace cleared his throat. "Well, we were running a sale last week on ladies' boots, twenty percent off. But I was telling my brother Homer this morning we should extend it another few days. He said it was fine by him."

She knew the man was fibbing, but it was a nice fib. She sat on a wooden stool to try on the boots. They fit right on her feet. She stretched her legs and rolled the boots on the back of their heels.

"They're awfully nice. I'll take them, too."

At the counter, Horace centered the glass shade on a stack of newspapers and wrapped the sheets to pad it. He tilted his head as he eyed Willi kindly.

"I was sad to hear of your little boy's death," he said. "We lost a child, too, a little girl, Pearl, our next to the youngest. She drowned in an irrigation pond. My wife thought I was watching her, and I thought she was. It was such a long time ago." He shook his head slowly. "It gets better, but you never forget. I don't think you're supposed to."

Willi smiled as she gazed into the man's eyes, a blue as light as water. Old-timers have manners, she thought, as she opened her purse to complete the purchase.

"I'm so sorry about your little girl," she said. "Yes, it's hard these days."

Moving On

An unfamiliar pickup was parked in front of the mobile home Junior shared with Sherry. Her car was beside it, and the lights were off except for the left side of the trailer where the wind had blown snow into a high bank beneath the bedroom windows. Junior stepped carefully over the mess the neighbors' mutts left on the front path before he opened the door, calling for Sherry as he walked toward their room.

He wasn't stupid. He knew what was going on, and he was right when he saw the naked backside of a man bouncing hard over Sherry. Strangely, the only feeling Junior had was gratitude. Sherry was making it easy for him, although he'd been hoping this thing they had would have lasted until he found another job this spring.

Junior coughed. "Don't mind me, folks."

The man rolled hurriedly off Sherry. Both sat up, yanking the sheets to their armpits. The guy looked like a jack-lit deer when he stared at Junior.

"Shit, Junior, you scared me. I wasn't expecting you back today," Sherry said.

Her eyebrows were pulled down in a worried way, but Junior wasn't planning to fight anyone. He raised his hand as if he were stopping traffic. He made a laugh.

"I can see that, honey. I'm just gonna get my things."

Junior found his duffle bags in the closet and began stuffing his clothing, dirty or clean, he could find. He recognized the guy from the bar where Sherry worked. *Their place*, she called it. He wasn't a bad guy, just a horny chump like him.

When Junior glanced back, the man was pulling on his jeans. Sherry's eyes sped from one man to another. Junior heard them argue when he went into the bathroom to get his shaving stuff. He was just about done, except for hitching the trailer for his snowmobiles to the back of his pickup. It was awfully cold to be doing this chore, but he'd never leave his rides behind.

Too Blue to Cry

Willi was jolted by the noise of so many people jammed inside the Pine Tree Tavern on a Saturday night. Smoke hung over their heads, and the jukebox played something twangy about, what else, a man with cheating on his mind. It was dry and cold outside with no sign of a warmup, so the carrying-on could be blamed rightfully on the tough, colorless winter.

She didn't feel the need to come, but Lorna thought differently. "For Christ's sake, Willi, you need to get out," she said when she stopped by her house. When Willi balked, Lorna threw her jacket and purse at her. "Let's go."

"Aw, Lorna, I don't wanna."

"Tough shit."

Her mother reminded Willi a couple of days ago she wasn't the only one in Hayward to have something bad happen.

"Do ya remember the little kid who died of cancer last year? How about that guy whose wife killed herself and left the pictures of him and his girlfriend spread all over their bed?"

"Gee, Ma, it ain't the same," Willi told her.

Since Cody's death, Willi preferred being locked away on her hilltop where the winter wind shook the windows of her house. When she came home from work, she carried in enough logs to feed the wood stove. Sometimes she found a show on TV she liked or she brought a magazine from the Lucky Lady. Other times she stood wrapped in a blanket, clutching something from her son. She gazed out a window, watching the wind scour the top dry layer of snow so fine the flakes lifted and swirled across the yard. She thought about the things she'd change. It wasn't hard. Daddy wouldn't have died. Ma wouldn't have married Joe. She would have given birth to a little boy who was right.

He wouldn't have slid into Miles Potter's truck.

Should she have married Junior? No, but she recalled how happy he could make her at the start. Junior was one of those dangerous men, handsome in a country way, the kind who come on strong to women with jokes and compliments. She should've married someone else, someone sweeter, someone truer, someone who would've loved her and her boy no matter what.

Willi squeezed past the guys jammed around the pinball machines at the Pine Tree. Lorna held a hand at the small of her back, prodding her to an empty table. She pointed to one near the dance floor. "This one, right here."

Lorna waved to two girls from the bakery where she worked and a guy, heavyset with a full, black beard. They came on snowmobiles, so they carried their helmets to the table. They unzipped their suits while Lorna made the introductions.

"Take your stuff off, and I'll get us some beers," Lorna said, and then she was gone.

Willi only came to the Pine Tree a few times since Pa died, when she got Lorna or her mom to watch Cody. One night she hooked up with a guy who followed her home in his pickup. He came over two other times, but on the last, Cody, sick with a cold, woke up fussy, so the man got scared off. She glanced around. He wasn't here.

Lorna lifted five bottles of Bud high as she wiggled through the crowd, stopping to say hello or make a wisecrack to the people she knew before she set the beers on the table. She slid one toward Willi. "Drink up."

The beer tasted so good; Willi warned herself not to drink too fast. She turned toward the back door when cold air drafting through its opening reached her. A group of men carried instruments and equipment to the bar's small stage.

"Gee, did the whole, damn town have to come tonight?" Lorna yelled in her ear.

The juke went thumpa-thumpa. Willi drank her beer, mustering a smile or a hello when someone recognized her. She saw Junior's brother Mike a few tables away. His on-again, off-again marriage must be off again because he talked closely with a dark-haired woman who wasn't his wife. Lorna was busy gossiping about people Willi didn't know, so she concentrated on the band getting ready.

One of Lorna's friends from the bakery set a fresh bottle of beer in front of her.

"My round next time," Willi said.

The band started its first song, something with a fast tempo. Willi tapped her foot as the four-piece band, The Loose Wheels, all local boys, made their way through a familiar tune, "Good Hearted Woman." Some of the men whooped their approval.

Willi glanced up when she saw a man standing in front of their table. It was Ray from the Hayward Garage, where she bought tires for her car this morning. He was tall and thin with dark hair he had combed back slick. Ray was one of the boys in her class at the Hayward Elementary School, and they went to the vocational high school together.

Ray gave her a lopsided grin. "How are those tires working out for you?"

"Oh, just fine. I had no trouble gettin' up my driveway tonight."

"The ones you had were really shot. I'm surprised you didn't get a flat."

Ray stood still. Willi thought she should ask him to sit down because he blocked her view of the band. "Is that your brother Roy up there?"

Ray nodded. The man playing rhythm guitar was his twin. She smelled the pomade on Ray's hair when he leaned toward her. "Wanna dance?"

"No, no thanks," Willi whispered.

But Lorna moved forward.

"Never mind her. I'll dance with you." Lorna grabbed Ray's hand and dragged him to the dance floor. She called over her shoulder. "Don't forget those beers, Willi."

Willi heard, but she stayed put, watching her sister take the lead on the dance floor. Lorna held Ray's hand, moving him every which way she jerked his arm. Willi giggled. Ray's eyes and mouth were so wide open, he looked as if he was going to bite her sister. The dance ended, but Lorna held onto Ray's hand, so he wouldn't escape. He blinked and shuffled his feet when the band began again. Willi laughed so hard, tears welled in her eyes. Lorna was right. She needed a little fun.

The line to the restroom was three-women deep, and after she was done in there, Willi went to the bar for the beers she promised Lorna. She found an empty space at the rail, where she asked the bartender, a friend of Daddy's, for five beers. The bartender kidded Willi about showing an ID, and when he popped the caps, a voice said, "Why don't you put those on my tab?"

Willi turned to her left. Miles sat two stools away in front of a bottle of Bud and an empty shot glass. His buddy, Dave was beside him. Miles smiled like she remembered he smiled, wide and with deep dimples in his cheeks. She walked toward him.

"That's awfully nice of you." She grinned back. "By the way, I used some of that money you left to buy new tires. Thank you."

"What money? I didn't leave you any money."

She stared at his hair. It hung crookedly, as if he had cut it himself, and now it was growing out.

"Yeah, you did." Her words were loose and too loud. "Gee, you need a haircut real bad."

"Miles, you look like some goddamn hippie," Dave joked. "Why don't you let her cut it for you?"

"Yeah, come on by," Willi said.

"That place in Tyler? The Lucky Lady? My mother went there. I don't think so."

Dave rolled his eyes. "Well, if you're gonna work for me hanging line, you gotta look your best. Willi, we'll be up your way tomorrow. I'm renting the doctor's sugar bush. See, here. I have it all mapped out." Dave pulled a paper folded in a neat square from his shirt pocket and spread it on the bar. He had drawn circles of varying sizes, connected by a pattern of lines, as neat as a draftsman's blueprint. "This is the doctor's hill. These circles are the maple trees. These lines are the tubing. See where they lead to this large vat?"

Willi gave the paper a peek, but her eyes stayed on Miles. "Stop boring her with that stuff, you pest," he said.

Giggling, Willi took a step closer to Miles. She remembered

how he could get her to laugh so easily when they were kids. It felt good again. She wanted to stay, but the song was winding down, and Lorna would be bothered if the beers were not at the table. She grabbed the bottles by their necks and smiled again at Miles.

"You're gonna be across the road? Well, if you get cold, stop by. Don't mind my dog, Foxy. She won't bite you. She's just a little faker."

"I'll remember that."

Back at the table, Lorna took a break. Ray, she said, went to the men's room. "He's a great dancer, don't you think?"

"Ray?"

Willi laughed so hard she put her bottle down.

"What's wrong with you, Willi?"

Lorna started laughing along with Willi, not because she knew what was funny, but because she had caught her sister's mood.

Willi tried several times to catch her breath. Finally, she blurted, "Well, yeah, 'cause he does everything you want him to."

Lorna made a dirty laugh. "Let's see what else he'll do for me."

"Lorna, you're awful."

Happy tears were in Willi's eyes. Then Ray was back, and Lorna gave him the once-over. "Okay, Ray, let's dance some more."

Willi thought about the music Daddy made, not as fine as Pa, whose fingers moved over his guitar as if they were a part of the instrument even when he was very old. Pa welcomed the attention his music brought him. He would have loved being on the stage with the band tonight but not Daddy. He only did it when Pa asked him.

She recalled the bashful smile Daddy wore when he was happy with his daughters. He let her and Lorna sit astride each thigh, jostling them as if they were riding a team of horses. They held onto his arms, shrieking as he bounced them in trots and gallops, such a loving father. But there were times when Daddy got so quiet Willi worried he didn't like their life. After she and

Lorna went to bed, Daddy took his guitar from its case, plucking and stroking its strings in a lonely country ballad. She crept from her room and positioned herself behind an easy chair to spy on her father. A bottle and shot glass were on the end table, and between each tune, he'd take a sip. One night, Willi ran to Daddy, begging him to sing something happy for her. She squeezed between him and his guitar, so he set the instrument on the floor. He pulled her onto his lap and kissed the top of her head.

"Oh, sweetheart," was all he said as he held her in his arms, but then after a long time, he whispered, "Now get down so I can play."

Daddy started singing "I'm in the Jailhouse Now," exaggerating his voice to make the tune sound funny. She stayed close, smiling so hard at Daddy he had to do the same with her.

Ma never talked about Daddy. "I'm married to Joe now," was all she'd say.

Willi didn't know how much her Daddy drank, but one night, it was enough to get him killed when he crashed his car. It was the only time Willi saw her mother cry. "What will I do with you two?" She said those words so sharply it scared Willi that their mother would leave them. Ma maybe did her best, but she was like a double-bladed knife missing its handle. There was a trick to holding it safely.

One of the musicians in Roy's band played the mandolin, which led into a wild redneck stomp that inspired the dancers. People were so drunk they bumped into each other. Willi's eyes kept coming back to her sister and sweet, dumb Ray.

One of Lorna's friends joked, "Didn't figure Ray had such moves."

"Neither did I," Willi told her.

Then Ray's brother Roy spoke into the microphone. "Here's a little somethin' from Hank," and he loosened his voice as he sang the opening to "I'm So Lonesome I Could Cry."

The couples who cared about each other started dancing close, even though it had to be the saddest song Hank Williams ever sang. The weight of its words pulled at Willi's heart. She shouldn't have come. A woman who lost her boy only a month ago had a nerve sitting in a bar. She should be home thinking about him.

Now, Willi's tears were real. She lowered her head. One of Lorna's friends asked if she was okay.

"I just need some fresh air," she whispered.

Willi stood, pulling on her coat, but leaving her purse behind. She stumbled against an empty chair but made it outside, where the cold hit her like a slap to the jaw. She took deep breaths, hoping the chill would sober her. What was she thinking about drinking beer so fast? She wasn't some high school kid.

She recognized Miles's truck, parked near a row of snowmobiles and walked slowly toward it. She stared at the dent on the driver's door and then reached to trace it with a fingertip.

"So small," she whispered.

"Yeah, it is."

Willi turned. Miles's voice so startled her, she felt as if she were losing her balance. She said his name.

"I'm sorry, Willi. I didn't mean to scare you."

"I'm all right," she said. "I was just lookin' at your truck."

"The dent. I'm gonna get it fixed soon. I can't stand seein it every day."

"Fixed."

Willi swayed a little, and Miles used an arm to steady her. She was crying again.

"I saw you go outside," he said. "I wanted to make sure you were okay."

"People keep sayin' things will get better."

"They have to, Willi."

Willi raised her eyes. The lines of Miles's face were soft. She touched his cheek and felt his sorrow, one sure thing they had in common. If someone who didn't know their story saw them together, they'd think they were readying for a kiss, but Willi was wiser. She decided she was sober enough to go back inside before Lorna came searching for her.

All Wrong

The next morning, close to noon, Willi tied a rope to Foxy's collar to take her for a walk. She used to let her go unleashed, but the doctor who had the place next door complained to the town's dog officer, who called her about it. The next time he picked up Foxy, Willi would have to pay to get her back. Foxy was a harmless mutt, but she could appear ill-tempered to people who didn't know her. Pa, who raised her from a pup, said she was just a bit bossy.

"Foxy likes keeping people in line. Just like your sister, Lorna," Pa joked.

Willi wore her new boots from Fishers Hardware. They were a little cumbersome for driving, but they had thick wool liners, so her feet would be warm enough finally, which was lucky since the sun, although bright, shed a hollow light today. She could cross having new boots off her to-buy list. Next, she would get a decent coat. The one she wore, something her mother found at the church rummage sale, didn't fit and its zipper stopped working a while ago. She yanked on her hat and gloves. The dog danced happy steps in the kitchen as Willi turned down the wood stove's damper.

When Willi got up this morning, the house was so cold the windows were thick with frost on the inside. She was too tired and drunk last night to fill the firebox after Lorna drove her home, so she slept in her coat and let the dog come on the bed. Her sister was in too giddy a mood, talking about what she and Ray would be doing at his place that she didn't complain about Willi drinking too much.

"I like a man who works with his hands," Lorna said in a tuneful voice.

Lorna didn't mention Miles.

Willi and Foxy walked up the driveway, and then hung a left onto Barker Road, called that because a famous writer by that name used to live in the doctor's house. It was such a long time ago, most people no longer read his poetry, but the town was proud of him still. The road was clear to the pavement, which meant Foxy could walk without snow and ice getting stuck in her paws. They passed Dave's pickup truck parked snugly against a snowbank on one side of the road. He and Miles were working on the sugar bush. Her eyes followed the tracks their snowshoes made up the hill. The dog barked when the two men's voices bounced upon the hillside.

"Shhh, it's okay, Foxy."

Somewhere on the hill Dave and Miles stretched tubing between the hill's sugar maple trees. She stood on tiptoes but couldn't see them. The dog paced and pulled the rope.

"Yeah, yeah, we're goin'."

A half-mile up the road, Willi came to the doctor's grand Colonial, which he had painted a creamy yellow last summer. The place was filled with antiques, including the famous writer's desk, which should be in a museum, Nathan, the caretaker, told her once with scorn.

She and Foxy reached the end of the road, where the plow truck pushed the snow back far and wide so there'd be a turnaround. The road was dirt beyond this point. Although still a legal way, it wasn't easily passable, and the town officially closed it for the winter. A state forest began where the doctor's property ended.

The summer before Pa died, he asked Willi to drive him this way in his truck, a lengthy route that took them roundabout through two other towns before they reached Tyler. She got nervous the truck would bottom out, and she'd have to back her way out, or something would happen to its undercarriage. But Pa kept saying, "You're doin' fine, Willi. This old truck sits high."

At one point, Pa asked her to stop the truck. She helped him and Cody into the woods, where her grandfather directed her to a grove of massive hardwoods, an old-growth forest, he explained. The three of them could hold hands and not reach around most of them. Some were three hundred years old, Pa told her. The writer who lived in the doctor's house wrote a poem about the trees when they were a hundred years younger.

"Nice to see somethin' older than me," Pa joked as he leaned against Willi.

Now, Willi let Foxy sniff the snowbank before she whistled to go back. When they passed the doctor's house again, he was outside, getting something from his Volvo station wagon. The doctor wore a ski jacket, a blue as bright as a jay's. He said hello when he noticed her, so she stopped. Foxy snapped her jaws in nasty little nips, but Willi gave the rope a tug, so the dog quieted.

"I was sorry to hear about your little boy. Such a tragedy."

"Yes, it is," Willi said slowly, embarrassed she used rope to hold her dog.

"If there's anything we can do, let us know." Willi knew he meant his wife, too, who waved if she saw her in her yard. "I liked your grandfather even though we could never make a deal on his house."

Willi felt something click inside. It seemed bad manners to bring up this topic considering what had happened, and she recalled her grandfather's words to never sell the doctor his house no matter how much.

"Well, Pa wanted *me* to have it. Sorry, I've gotta go. I'm gettin' cold standing here."

Willi stopped when she reached Dave's pickup. The hill was steep, and Dave was figuring on using gravity to let the sap flow to the plastic tank he would set at the bottom. There was no sign sap would begin running soon. Snow wrapped high and tight around the tree trunks like a preacher's collar. Their limbs appeared lifeless. The weather had yet to moderate into that pattern of above-freezing temperatures during the day and below at night.

Willi was near her driveway when she heard the drone of a snowmobile. A trail ran across the doctor's lower field where it left the woods for a brief section a mile from her house. Someone was off course, or maybe it was Nathan checking the doctor's fence. She remained still as the machine crossed the boundary of maples onto her land. The rider was dressed in black, and sunlight glinted off the helmet's shield. Her heart began a fearful ache. She called the dog and quickened her pace back to the house.

The machine parked in her driveway. When the driver removed his helmet, she saw he was Junior. A grin lifted his heavy mustache.

"Hey, there, Willi," he said.

Foxy charged at Junior, but Willi held onto the rope. "What do you want?"

Junior kept calling her at night, so she stopped answering her phone unless she heard a welcomed voice on the message machine.

His words were the same each time: "Call me, Willi. I wanna talk with you."

Junior removed his gloves and smoothed his hair back with a bare hand. In the sunlight, she saw it was beginning to gray.

"Aw, Willi. I came to tell you I'm sorry."

His voice was tender and smooth, but he wasn't fooling her. She frowned at Junior as the dog kept up her wild barking. "Stay there, Junior. I'll be back."

She coaxed Foxy to calm down as she led her into the house. "Good girl, Foxy," she murmured, when she shut the dog inside.

Junior waited beside his snowmobile. Willi recalled the few times he came here to see Cody when Pa was still alive. Her grandfather sat in his recliner, giving Junior a close watch while Cody hid behind the chair. She and Junior quickly ran out of things to talk about. He rubbed his face and yawned before he left a half-hour later.

Willi stopped in front of her ex-husband. She crossed her arms. "What was it you wanted to tell me?"

Junior cleared his throat.

"When I saw that picture of our boy, I realized how much he looked like me." He stopped. "I was a real lousy father to him. I know it now." He lowered his head briefly. "Do you remember how happy I was when he was born? Believe me, I was. When we found out about him not being right, I just couldn't handle it." His voice trailed off. "I stopped thinking about him and you. I was wrong, all wrong."

Willi wrapped her coat, so it closed around her. She was chilled now that she wasn't moving. "You're a little late, aren't you?"

Junior shifted from one boot to another. "Shit, Willi, I just wanna make it up to you."

"Is that so?"

She glared at Junior. She remembered how she and Cody used to eat spaghetti with margarine for supper while he was out chasing women. If it hadn't been for Pa, she didn't know what she would've done.

"I wanna show you somethin'," she told Junior.

Willi marched around the side shed and toward the backyard. The snow reached her boot tops, but she kept going until she got to the clothesline. Junior was behind her.

"Stop right here," she said.

Willi used her hand to guide Junior's line of vision over the hill's steep edge. It snowed since the accident, but she still could make out where her feet sank as she tried to catch her boy. Her prints formed a dotted seam, which made it seem as if the earth could split easily along that line.

"See that?"

Junior squinted at her pointed finger. "What am I lookin' at?"

"That's where it happened. That's where Cody died. How do you think you're gonna make that up to me?"

Willi sobbed loudly, and she didn't care if Junior saw or heard her. His hands were stretched out, palms up, as if he were surrendering. Junior said her name as he came closer, but Willi took a swing, catching him on his face in one solid shot that made him grunt. She collapsed, sobbing and pounding the snow with her fists. Junior came close again, but this time she didn't resist. She let him help her to her feet and use his arm to guide her into the house.

The dog charged the door, threatening to bite Junior. Willi told the animal to stay as she walked toward the couch.

"Here, let me get your coat," Junior said, and she stood

passively as he slipped the bulky black cloth off her and threw it on a chair. "You gonna be okay?"

She didn't answer, but lay back on the couch. Her eyes fluttered.

"I think so." Her voice was barely above a whisper. "I feel so tired. Just leave."

"Right, I have to get somewhere."

"Then, go."

Junior got up to feed wood into Willi's stove. He brought more from the shed, stacking the logs near the stove, now hot enough to turn down. He stood in the living room. His eyes traveled the room. She knew he was staring at Cody's things.

"Willi, listen to me. I wanna pay the money I owe you. Just tell me how much."

She watched him with sleepy eyes.

"It was never just the money. We needed you."

Junior exhaled deeply and mumbled, "yeah," as he went for the door.

Nothing Happened

The next day after work, Willi carried a cardboard box through her mother's house. She called for her while she went from the kitchen to the living room, where she found Joe asleep on the couch. The TV blared, but her stepfather snored with his mouth open. He had an afghan spread over him, although the house was as hot as a nursing home, the way Joe, who worked outside liked it. He complained that hauling hose from the propane truck through thigh-deep snow permanently chilled him.

Her fight yesterday with Junior inspired her to finally pack up Cody's things. Then she cried when she was finished.

Willi had two more boxes in the car. Ma had said last night when she called that she could store them in the attic. She'd be home, but she wasn't. Only Joe was here. She turned to leave, but Joe stirred.

"What's goin' on?" he growled.

Joe pulled back the afghan, wincing as he moved into a sitting position. He wore a white t-shirt, stained yellow around the armpits. He sucked snot to the back of his throat, and then swallowed it.

"I was just bringing some of Cody's stuff. Ma said I could put it in the attic."

His fingernails scraped over his whiskers. "Oh, she did, did she? You got a lot of junk to bring in?"

She shook her head as she held the box closer. "What are you doin' home? I didn't think you'd be here."

"Yeah, well, I slipped on some ice at work and twisted my ankle this morning. Swelled up like a son of a bitch. Doc said I should be out for a couple of days." He tugged the blanket, so she saw the bottom of his hairy leg raised on a pillow. An ice pack was near the ankle. "Say, how about gettin' me a beer?"

Willi shifted the box to her right hip. Gunfire and shouting came from the TV set.

"Where's my mother?"

"She went to the drugstore to get my pills. How about that beer? Jesus, Willi, my ankle hurts like hell."

She set the box on the coffee table and went to the kitchen. An unopened twelve pack of Bud was in the refrigerator.

"Help yourself," he shouted.

Willi brought only one can into the living room. She held it in front of her stepfather, but he grasped her wrist instead. She jerked her arm, but he held on tightly.

"Bet you weren't expectin' me to be here, did you? Huh?" He made a sly smile. "What do you say, sweetheart?"

She gave Joe a hard stare. "Get your fuckin' hand off me."

He jumped when she dropped the unopened can of beer in his lap. "Shit, Willi, whatcha do that for? Nothin' happened."

"There's the beer you wanted."

Willi backed away from his reach. She felt overheated in her coat, but she wasn't about to take it off.

"So I hear, Missy. You're gonna be sitting pretty."

"What do you mean?"

"The insurance money. Lorna told us all about it. The one you got at school, where they pay you so much if your kid loses an eye or dies."

Willi shook her head. "I'm not getting any money. The school insurance cost twenty bucks. I didn't have twenty bucks for that. Maybe if Junior paid child support for Cody, I could've."

"Yeah, yeah, be that way, after all your mother did for you."

She crossed her arms. "Shut up, Joe. You dunno what you're talkin' about as usual."

"Talkin' about what?" Her mother came quickly beside her. She held a white bag that rattled when she shook it. "Got the pills. Joe, you're not supposed to drink with 'em. Willi, you shouldn't have given him that beer."

"Who the fuck cares?" Joe growled. "Just give 'em to me."

Her mother swung around, but neither she nor Joe answered.

"What's goin' on?" she asked.

99

Willi lifted the box. "We just had a few words. Right, Joe?"

Joe was silent.

Ma pressed her lips together. Deep creases formed between her eyes.

"What you got there, Willi?" she asked.

"Cody's things. I was gonna leave 'em here, but I changed my mind. I've got plenty of room back at my place."

Willi looked at Joe. If his glare were any stronger, it would've knocked her to the floor.

"Why don't you stay, Willi?" her mother said. "I was just gonna fix us somethin' to eat."

"Nah, I gotta get goin'."

Ma followed her through the kitchen to the back door. Willi turned around. Ma's scowl pinched her face. "I wish you'd make more of an effort with Joe. Lorna does. Think of me, Willi."

She shifted the box as her mother got the door's knob.

"Believe me, Ma, I always do."

Outside, Willi followed the cleared walkway to her car. She set the box in the back seat with the others. She thought she heard a new noise in the engine when she started the car.

"Nothing happened," she said to herself.

The first time she was thirteen. Joe offered to pick her up after a birthday party. She was so happy to stay that late. She thought nothing of it when Joe took the back way home, but then he parked his truck in the entrance of a logging road in a remote part of Hayward. He cut the headlights.

"Willi, I've been watchin' you. You're a pretty girl, but I don't think you know it. I like that in a girl."

Joe's voice was as warm as he made it for her mother. He stretched his hand to stroke one finger against her cheek. Willi's heart started harder. She slid against the door. She wished she didn't wear shorts and a tank top because Joe stared at her bare parts.

"Come here, you," he said.

"No, I wanna go home."

Joe leaned forward and grabbed the upper part of her arms. He tried to kiss her, but she twisted away, so his whiskers burned her lips. He got her the second time, forcing his sour tongue inside her mouth, working it hard in a way she had never been kissed. His broken front tooth was so sharp, she was afraid it would cut her.

"Come on, Willi. I'm not gonna hurt you."

Joe worked his belt buckle loose, and then the front of his pants. His hand reached inside his shorts, and when he pulled it out, it looked like he was grasping a dark, ready thing.

She turned away fast so she wouldn't have to see it.

Joe laughed from the back of his throat. "Never seen one before, eh? Wanna touch it? Nah?"

Willi couldn't speak, so instead she closed her eyes, locking herself away where he couldn't reach her. He was breathing hard and grunting. She cried out when he grabbed her bare thigh, wanting to get out of his way, but he had her pinned against the door. Joe looked as if he was choking. She hoped he was dying, but then he let out a yell. His fingers gripped her thigh tighter. Then Joe was on his side of the truck.

"I wouldn't tell your mother about this, if you know what's good for you and for her. I'm the one who keeps this home goin'." His voice had been hard and low. "That's right. Nothin' happened to you. You were only here."

That night, Willi walked straight to her room and shut the door without saying a word to her mother. She understood the threat. Joe would leave, and they'd be poor again. Her mother would never forgive her for that. But she couldn't forgive Joe for what he did. Ever. No man should do things like that to a girl who's supposed to be his stepdaughter.

Joe started sneaking home early when he knew her mother was still at work or when he came into her room at night, she'd wake to see him staring down at her.

"Please don't make me," she cried.

Then he'd laugh.

Her mother didn't understand why she moved in with her cousins a few days after she graduated from high school. How could she say, "I hate the man you married?"

Willi put the car in gear. When she glanced back, her mother's face was in the window. Ma wasn't smiling.

Uphill

Miles crouched on his snowshoes high above the doctor's hill. Dave stood to his left, studying his map and appraising the pattern of maple trees on the slope below them. No one had tapped this sugar bush in years, but Dave told Miles it didn't take much to convince the doctor it'd be a worthwhile use of his land. He said he would even hang some covered metal buckets, although no one ever used them anymore, on the roadside trees to make the way look scenic. Dave was paying him off with syrup. He said the doctor liked the idea of giving jugs of maple syrup from his trees to his friends in New York.

They were two-thirds of the way done stringing the purple-colored tubing connecting each tree to a main line. When the job was done, they'd return to drill holes and set the taps. Many of the trees would have two or three, depending on their girth.

Dave was one of those newcomers who fell in love with everything the old-timers didn't do anymore. Setting line was cold work, but Dave kept at it in a cheerful pace. Most of the time Miles concentrated on what his friend was telling him to do or pulling the line taut between the trees, grateful for the deliverance of hard work. This was their third day at it, and although he kept his bar stool at the Pine Tree, he found it easier to fall asleep afterward.

Dave folded the map in quarters and tucked it into the back pocket of his jeans. They were losing light, but it being February, the day was getting a bit longer. Dave leaned for a roll of tubing.

"This is gonna be a great year. I can feel it in my bones," Dave said.

"That's what you said last year. Then, we had that spring

102

heat wave, and it was all over. Remember?"

"Hey, don't burst my bubble. I like doing this."

The two friends worked up and down the hill like a team of reliable farmhands, swapping stories when they stopped for a break. Dave talked about his kids. Miles told him about building bluebird houses for Linwood.

"I messed up the first but got the rest done reasonably well," Miles said. "When I brought them to Linwood's house, the son of a gun checked each one over like he had ordered fine furniture."

"That sounds like something Linwood would do," Dave said.

"When he pulled out his wallet, I told him I wasn't charging him. Shit, Dave, you know what Linwood said? 'Miles, nothing free is ever good enough.' Can you beat that?"

Miles straightened his legs. The snowshoes held him to the slope. They belonged to Dave. They weren't made of rawhide and wood like the ones his mother hung on the walls of their den, but aluminum and plastic, with a metal claw that moved beneath the balls of his feet. They crunched loudly as they broke through the crusty snow, but they gripped the surface well and gave him a better turning radius than the old-fashioned kind. He thought of asking Dave if he could borrow a pair, so he could hike the snowmobile trails near his home.

Their position on top of the hill gave them a wide-angle view of the Mercy River's valley and, in particular, Willi's yard. Her small, square house seemed crushed by the doctor's property. A green junker, the pickup truck that belonged to her grandfather, was half-buried in snow. So was the doghouse where Willi's fierce little mutt roamed as far as her chain allowed. The dog knew they were up there because she barked whenever he and Dave talked.

The temperature moderated today, a positive sign, Dave said, so they were on the hill this morning before Willi went to work. They stopped when they heard her car's engine. There was so little traffic on the road they couldn't help but notice.

On Sunday, Miles and Dave witnessed Junior's arrival on his snowmobile and what must have been an argument between him and Willi. Her voice rose to the hill, and he saw her take a swipe at her ex-husband. Miles was ready to charge down the hill, but he stopped when Junior helped her into the house. Junior left on his snowmobile not long afterward.

The two men hoisted rolls of tubing over each shoulder before they made their descent. They were halfway down when Willi's blue car barreled up the road, and then into her driveway. Miles heard the car door creak and slam. Willi walked in choppy movements through the snow toward her dog.

"What's going on down there?" Dave asked. "She all right?"

"I hope so," Miles said.

"The other day I was thinking about the time in second grade when the teacher started screaming about a spider crawling on her desk. Remember? Willi just walked up and pounded it flat with her fist."

Miles snorted. "I remember."

"She had guts," Dave said.

"She still does."

Miles recalled Willi didn't speak for a long time after her father died in the crash. She seemed pinched by the loss, wearing the same wounded expression she's held since Cody died. Willi was a person who felt deeply about things. She was someone who cared. He admired that.

Dave nudged Miles with his elbow. "What do you think she saw in Junior?"

"I suspect it was love," Miles answered.

When they reached the bottom of the hill, Willi appeared at the top of her driveway, wearing a floppy black coat. Her mutt charged forward, but stopped a few feet from Miles, where she calmed as he sweet-talked the dog. The frown on Willi's face melted when she recognized them. She crossed the road.

"How's the work goin', boys?" she asked.

"Dave's a real slave driver," Miles said.

"That's 'cause you've gotten soft on me," Dave said back.

Willi turned from one man to the other as they joked. If Willi was upset before, Miles was pleased to see how at ease she seemed now. He threw the roll of tubing onto the bed of Dave's truck. Snowflakes, tight and dry, began to fall.

"I wouldn't mind getting that haircut if the offer is still good," Miles said.

Willi lifted her eyes. "Yeah, of course, the offer's still good. Why don't you park your truck in my driveway while I go ahead? I need to check my mailbox first."

"Sure enough."

Miles whistled as he got into the cab of his truck. Ahead of him, near the end of her drive, Willi peered into the mailbox on its post but left empty-handed.

True Nature

Willi and Miles ate the chicken stew she made and rolls from Lorna's bakery. She insisted they eat before she started with his hair. "Or else you'll be hearing my stomach growl next to your ear," she said.

Miles glanced up from his bowl. "This stew is really tasty, Willi."

Smiling, she let her head fall.

"It's only stew and bread."

"Yeah, but it's better than anything I make."

"I cooked it last night," she said. "I boiled a whole chicken in a pot on the wood stove until it fell apart. That's the way Pa showed me. But I stuck to potatoes instead of the turnips he liked. I used lots of pepper."

Miles rolled the sleeves of his red flannel shirt to his elbows and pushed the cuffs of his thermal up his forearms. His boots stood next to hers beside the back door. He looked at home across the table when he spooned the stew into his mouth. Willi, Pa, and Cody always ate together. After her grandfather died, she and her boy shared supper. Now, it'd become a lonely spot in her day.

Miles raised his eyebrows. "Aren't you going to eat?"

"Uh-huh. There's more if you want. I always make enough to last a couple of days."

The dog snored at her spot beside the wood stove. Foxy settled down after Miles came inside the house, and Willi fed her.

Miles ran his hand over the surface of the tabletop. "This table's pretty old. See the tight grain of this pine?"

"It was Pa's. Practically everything in here was his." She glanced around. "We didn't have much when he moved us in."

Miles leaned back in his chair. "He was a neat old guy."

"Pa was the best. After Junior left, I had Uncle Boyd, Pa's brother, sell my stuff, piece by piece, at his auction barn. I made him promise not to tell Pa, but he did anyway. Pa just showed up one Sunday. He said, 'Willi, it'll be real easy to move you, so why don't we do it today.' And we moved just like that."

Willi ate for a while. She raised her eyes when Miles called her name.

"You all right there, Willi?"

She nodded.

"I was thinking about Pa. Cody was sick, and I was singin' to him, waitin' for the medicine to take away the pain in his ears. Pa was so mad at Junior and Ma for not helpin' us." She lifted the spoon to her mouth but put it back in the bowl. "Pa said hard times show a person's true nature. I know now he's right."

Willi looked directly at Miles. The corners of his lips curled upward.

The lights in the house dimmed briefly. The wind drove snow sideways, fanning it across the windowpanes like smoke. Willi went to the kitchen counter and brought an oil lamp to the table. She lit the wick inside the globe, its light casting a yellow shine on Miles.

"Just in case. The snow's comin' down hard. Maybe I should cut your hair, so you can head home."

Miles shook his head.

"No hurry."

"But the snow."

He raised his hand.

"What's a little snow?"

"You know, Miles, when you went to college, I didn't think you'd come back. I figured you'd be a lawyer or a doctor. Not banging nails for a living back here."

"I like banging nails for a living."

His voice set Willi's heart in a happy roll, but she worried since her road was the last to get plowed. She brought their dishes to the sink and went to the bathroom to retrieve scissors, a comb, hand mirror, and a towel. She insisted they start.

"I'm sorry I don't have a proper drape to keep the hair off your clothes," she said.

"That's not a problem."

Miles slid his chair away from the kitchen table, so Willi would have room. He slipped off his shirts, tossing them onto the back of the couch so casually, it seemed he did this all the time in front of her. His torso and arms were winter white and muscular, like most men who used their bodies to work. She smelled the sweat beneath his arms.

Willi laughed. "I can't cut your hair like that. Here, let me put this on you."

She wrapped the towel around his neck and pulled a safety pin from her pocket. His breath was warm against the skin of her arm as she pinned it in place.

Miles stretched back in his chair, his long legs crossed at the ankles. Willi gently combed a strand of wiry, brown hair on the lower back of his head. The tip of her scissors cut slowly across the ends. She let the hair fall to the floor. She chose another piece.

He hummed along with the radio, an old Johnny Cash tune she hadn't heard in a long time, the sound coming from deep in the man's chest. If Miles were a customer at the Lucky Lady, Willi would work quickly, making small talk, but instead she lingered as if each stand needed special attention. She knew Miles should leave because of the storm, but she wanted to prolong his departure.

"Remember the time this fall when we met outside the general store?" she asked. "It was Halloween and Cody was wearing a tiger suit I sewed for him. Well, only the body though 'cause he wouldn't wear the head. It scared him. But he let me draw whiskers on his face with my eyebrow pencil."

"Yeah, I remember that."

"You patted Cody's head and said, 'Who's this tough guy?'"

Her boy swiped his hand toward Miles like it had claws. He made a joyous howl.

108

"You remember what else you said? You called him a cute kid." She snipped another strand. "Hardly anybody ever called my son that."

"As I recall, he was a very cute kid."

She ruffled the part she cut with her fingertips. Miles sighed heavily. She could see from the mirror on the table his eyelids were heavy. His lips hung in a smile. She brushed bits of hair from the towel. Dark curls fell to the floor.

"You have such nice thick hair."

Willi stepped back to appraise her workmanship. She felt herself smile.

"I'm done." She placed her scissors and comb on the table. "I left it a little long like you wanted. Here, see if you like it this way."

She handed him the mirror and bent to unpin the towel. Miles checked his image.

"That's a great haircut all right."

Miles placed the mirror on the table. He wrapped his hand around her wrist. His soft touch surprised her, and she held her breath as he brought her hand to his mouth to kiss it. Gusts of wind sprayed the windows with hard flakes. He kissed her hand again, lightly, and she felt happy and sad at the same time.

Sharp gusts of wind rattled the windows.

"You'd better get goin', Miles. The roads are gonna be bad," she whispered.

He sighed again. "You sure?"

Willi felt her chest rise and fall. She knew where this moment could go.

"Yeah. You should go."

His fingers slipped from her wrist. His eyes stayed with hers. "Okay, I will then."

Willi went for his shirts draped over the chair. With her back to Miles, she used a finger to wipe tears from each eye. She took a deep breath before she turned.

"Here you go," she said, and then softer, "maybe some other time."

Miles nodded.

"I'd like that, Willi."

Junior's Plan

Across town at the Pine Tree Tavern, Junior had it all worked out. At least that's what he told Mike as they sat at a table. The two brothers had burgers, and now they drank beer. Junior felt pretty good. He was delivering propane, the temporary job his father told him about, and for now, he was living at his mother's. He had a lead on an apartment at that firetrap in town, the Wayward Hayward. It wasn't much, but it could be home. He and Willi used to live there.

"Maybe I'll join you," Mike said. "Dee threatened to throw me out last night. I might have to call her bluff."

"Jesus, not again. How many kids you got? Three? What in the hell you thinkin' about, little brother?"

"You should talk, big brother."

"Yeah, I fucked up. I'll admit it. But I'm gonna pay back every cent I owe Willi."

Mike slapped the edge of the table. "All of it? Are you nuts? How much you owe her?"

"Not a clue."

Junior paid what the court ordered for almost a year, but then he slacked off. How was he supposed to live the life he wanted if he had to give Willi and the boy so much of his paycheck? For a long while she hounded him, but she stopped after she moved in with her grandfather. He figured the old man was taking care of them.

"Well, I plan to give her the seven hundred I got on me and pay her a little each month."

His brother laughed like he heard a dirty joke. "Yeah, how long is that gonna last?"

"Shut up, Mike. Can't I do anything right in this family for once?"

The bar was filling up, mostly players from the Tuesday night pool league and their fans. The Pine Tree's team was hosting one from the county seat, he knew, because the owner joked earlier whether they'd be able to find their way to Hayward in the snow.

Mike lit a cigarette.

"Huh, I bet you dunno Lorna brought Willi here Saturday night," he said on the exhale. "Yeah, that's right. And who do you think I saw talkin' with her? Miles Potter. And get this, afterwards I saw her run outside crying. Then, he went after her. Wonder what that was all about."

Junior's jaw felt tight. He was interested in what Mike had to say. The cops said the accident wasn't Miles's fault, but he should've seen his boy coming down the hill. He could've done something to stop it.

"What the hell was he doin' bothering Willi?" Junior growled. "We ought a fix that asshole good."

The ridge of Mike's forehead rose. "I've got a way."

Junior reached for Mike's pack and shook out a butt. "Yeah, what?"

"I heard he's been workin' on that house on the hill for those rich New Yorkers."

"So?"

"Guess who's the contractor? Our cousin Benny."

Junior snickered as he flicked the lighter.

"Maybe I guess it's time I give ol' Cousin Benny a call."

Never Change

Willi stooped to pick another log from the load of firewood her neighbor, Nathan delivered while she was at work. Another storm was expected tomorrow, maybe a foot of snow, her customers said this afternoon, and tonight the full moon bore a telltale lacy ring. She muttered curses as she moved the logs inside the shed.

She filled the shed this fall with three cords she bought from Nathan, stacking them in two high and stable rows. Cody stayed near her, laughing when he heard the wood fall clop-clop upon each other.

Willi was afraid she'd run out of wood before spring. Pa used to say by Christmas you should have burned no more than half your supply, but that didn't happen this winter. She kept the woodstove, her only source of heat, going constantly since late October. Cody, who was sick on and off through the holidays, needed the house extra warm. The past few weeks she tried making the pile stretch, but it just got too cold at night. She had to let the water run a bit in the kitchen and bathroom faucets so the pipes wouldn't freeze. When she called, Nathan said he could spare a cord of dry wood, delivered for a fair price.

She worked at the beauty shop until four, passing Miles and Dave as they were leaving. Miles came over when she stopped her car. He leaned inside her open window, wearing the fresh smell of someone who'd been outside all day. She checked the progress of their lines on the doctor's hill.

"Looks like you're almost done," she told Miles.

"Well, hopefully, the sap will start running soon, and when that happens, we'll be back every day with the truck. For Dave's sake, I hope it lasts a while." He grinned big for her.

"Don't worry. You're not getting rid of me so soon."

"Stop by anytime," she told him.

"Don't worry. I will," he told her back.

Willi's trips between the woodpile and shed were short and deliberate. She couldn't afford to lose the wood in the snow. Lorna's beater Ford barreled up the driveway when Willi left the shed for another load. The car's headlights swept over her. She was glad to see her sister, although Lorna would not pitch in for this dirty chore. She had other plans tonight. Willi heard about them over the phone.

Lorna pulled a loaf of bread from a grocery bag. "Hey, Willi, I brought you some stuff from the bakery. Got you some sticky buns and half a pie, too."

"Thanks. So, tell me Lorna is that all the stuff you dropped on the floor today?"

"Very funny, wise guy."

Willi sniffed at her sister. "What's that I smell? Perfume?"

"Maybe." She checked her watch. "Hey, I gotta get goin'. I sure hope Ray remembered to get more rubbers."

"Lorna!"

"What can I tell you? The man sure can make a woman sing." Lorna made a sneaky laugh, and Willi said her name again. "What's the matter? When's the last time you got laid?"

Willi playfully smacked her sister's arm, and Lorna yelped in fun. "None of your business."

"That long, eh?"

Willi carried more logs into the shed. Her sister followed closely behind. The rat living in the woodpile scurried along its bottom edge. Willi jumped back, bumping Lorna.

"Hey, watch it!" Lorna said.

"Sorry. There's a rat in the shed. I can't stand the thing."

Willi dropped the logs onto the stack.

"I'll ask Joe to shoot it for you," Lorna said.

Willi spun around. Her frown pulled at the features of her face. "I'd rather live with a rat."

"Jesus, Willi, what's between you two? If I mention your name around the house, Dad, I mean Joe, bites off my head." She scowled. "Is it 'cause of the insurance thing? I told you

113

already I'm sorry I brought it up. I was wrong about that."

Willi eyed Lorna. The bare bulb hanging from the shed's rafter whitened her sister's face unnaturally. She told no one about Joe, not even Junior. She couldn't. She was too ashamed.

"Can I ask you a question?" Willi waited until her sister nodded. "Did any of the men in our family ever touch you or do somethin' they weren't supposed to?"

Lorna hooted. "What? Are you crazy? Where in the hell did you get an idea like that?"

Willi shrugged.

"I read about it in a magazine from the Lucky Lady." She kept her eyes on Lorna. "That's okay, Lorna. Just thought I'd ask. You never know these days."

"I suppose."

Her sister left minutes after she put the bag of food in the house. Willi continued bending and carrying wood. She took off her jacket when she got too hot from the work. She had a rhythm going, so she didn't feel like letting Foxy, who was howling about something, off her chain. Willi raised her head when she heard a truck's large motor move up the hill of Barker Road, and then into her drive. The headlights of a propane truck blinded her. The motor stopped. Then, Junior hopped down from the cab, yelling hello. He snapped the front of his canvas vest.

"Willi, what the hell are you doin' in the dark?"

"I'm bringin' in this wood. We're supposed to get more snow tomorrow."

"Here. Let me give you a hand."

"You don't have to."

But Junior loaded his arms with wood and walked her path into the shed. "I thought you were runnin' low the other day. This stuff good and dry. Where d'you get it?"

She stooped for more logs. "I bought it from Nathan next door."

Junior continued to help, bringing in twice the amount Willi could carry, whistling and making comments about the town and its people. She wasn't interested in the town's business,

114

although she heard plenty at the Lucky Lady and from her mother about what its people were up to, typically no good.

"Heard one a guy on the highway crew flipped a dump truck," Junior said. "I bet the road boss must be pissed."

She was grateful not to do this job alone although it bugged her, his acting so cheerful, as if they were married and happily doing a household chore together. The question lingered. What did Junior want?

A pack of coyotes yipped from their spot on the ridge above the doctor's house. They set Foxy barking again.

"What's that mean little mutt of yours up to?"

Willi giggled. "Fixin' to bite you, I suppose."

The corner of Junior's mouth twitched in a half-smile beneath his mustache. "I wouldn't put it past her."

The job done, Willi stretched to pull the light bulb's chain, but she stepped back as the rat moved again. Junior saw it too. He grabbed a barn shovel leaning against the wall and slammed it over the fleeing animal. Blood and pieces of the rat were left on the dirt floor when he lifted the shovel.

"Shit, I hate rats," Junior said.

He used the shovel to scoop up the animal. From the shed's doorway Willi saw him fling the rat's carcass far from the house, then dip the shovel's bloody end into the snow before he brought the tool back to its place. Willi would've forced herself to kill the rat if Cody were still here. She would never have asked Junior to do it, but she was glad he did.

Junior stood there as she thanked him. The ball in his throat went up and down. She knew his ways. He had something to say. "Junior, why'd you come here?"

"I wanna give you somethin'. Can we go inside? It's cold as hell."

"Yeah, it's cold. Come on."

She grabbed her coat and a couple of logs. Junior followed with an armload.

Inside, he halted before setting the wood beside the stove.

"You packed all his things," he said.

Willi sighed.

"Yeah, I did it the other night. It was too depressing seeing

115

his toys everywhere, like he was gonna play with 'em again. Now, the house feels real empty."

Junior walked toward Cody's bedroom. He paused, giving Willi a backward glance, and after she nodded, he went inside. She followed him as far as the doorway. The three boxes she brought back from Ma's were on the floor. The jar of Cody's ashes and the framed school photo belonging to her mother were on the dresser. Junior sank into the bare mattress's striped ticking. He played with the ends of his mustache.

"You might not wanna sit there." Her voice thinned to a whisper. "Cody used to wet the bed sometimes. I have to haul it to the dump this spring when they bring back the open-top container."

"I can take it in my truck if you like."

"If you're still here."

Junior's eyelids nearly closed.

"You really hate my guts, don't you, Willi?" She didn't answer. "I guess you've got your reasons." He removed his wallet from the back pocket of his jeans. He stood facing her. "I told you I was gonna pay you back. Here's a start. Seven hundred."

Willi studied Junior's face as he held the bills. He seemed sincere, but she wasn't buying it. In time, Junior would be the same old Junior, slick and loose, thinking of himself first. He was only trying to make himself feel better because Cody died. But he did owe her money. She wouldn't refuse.

She took the bills.

"I haven't figured out how much you owe me yet. But as you said, this is a start, a real good start, Junior."

He liked what he heard, she knew, because he grinned broadly. "I gotta head out. Meetin' Mike. I only stopped to give you the money, but then I saw you needed help."

"I sure did."

He left, and afterward, Willi went outside to get Foxy. With the full moon, she didn't need a flashlight. The dog ran in circles as they returned to the house, crossing the path where her and Junior's feet trampled the snow into a compact layer.

The dog sniffed the dirt floor inside the shed where Junior

killed the rat.

"Come on. It's gone. Junior killed it."

Inside, she tuned the radio to the local Country and Western station. It was yet another sad song about love gone wrong. This time the man begged the woman to come back, but she wasn't so sure since it happened before. The dog followed her to the kitchen sink since it was time for her to eat. Willi lifted the bowls from the floor.

"Don't do it," she said out loud to the singer. "Don't be so stupid. He'll never change."

What It Would Take

The moonlight off the snow was so bright Junior could have driven without the truck's headlights. Little pictures played inside his head about Willi, their boy, the things he did or didn't do. These days they came without warning. When it happened, he tried to clear his head, but the pictures came faster. His chest felt tight and busy, like he drank too much coffee.

Right now, he thought about his first time with Willi. It was in September, that year as hot as late July. Softball season was done, but he and Willi still saw each other, going places and eating out. That night when they went for a ride, she sat close to him in his pickup, and the wind filling the open windows blew her long hair against his neck. He turned up the radio when a song she liked came on the station.

They ended up at a lake in Jarvis.

"Let's go for a swim," Junior told her.

"I don't have my bathing suit."

"Well, neither do I. But that's not stopping me."

She spread a blanket on the shore while he hurriedly stripped with his back to her, and then he made a shallow dive into the lake. When he came to the surface, she sat there, leaning back against her elbows. The moon was close to full, so he saw her clearly. He teased her about the water's cool temperature, how swell it felt. Junior was floating on his back when Willi got to her feet. He held his breath as she removed her clothing, starting at the top until moonlight glowed upon her skin. She hesitated for a moment but then stepped toward the water's edge. His eyes stayed on Willi as she came his way. The lake rose up her body until its waters held her breasts aloft.

She touched his outstretched hand.

"Jesus, Willi. You're so beautiful."

He began kissing her. At that moment, the lake could have dried up, and he wouldn't have noticed. He lifted Willi in his arms to bring her to the blanket where she let him have her.

Junior had been with many women before and after Willi, but none came close to what she gave him in their years together. He wondered what it would take to make her feel that way again.

The Reckoning

Miles planned to have a few beers at the Pine Tree, then go home, because he and Dave were heading to the doctor's hill early to finish hanging line. It was going to snow tomorrow, although the man sitting on the barstool to his right said the storm might move to the south of Hayward, a lucky miss, perhaps only a couple of inches after all. Even so, Dave had two more sugar bushes to fix.

It appeared as if Miles would be working indefinitely with Dave after the contractor called late last night with bad news. The job was off. When Miles pressed for details, the man got vague. Something was up. The couple loved his work.

Now, Miles worked for Dave at a third of his hourly rate. But there was merit to tromping through the snow, using nature in a righteous way, as his friend liked to put it. Dave lifted his spirit when he talked about being a steward of the land. His friend noticed things Miles had stopped seeing like animal tracks in the snow and the patterns of tree bark. Yesterday, Dave picked a maple leaf so dried and stripped it looked like a ragged piece of veil.

"Ever see anything like this before?" Dave had asked.

"I probably walk on them all the time," he answered.

Besides, Miles enjoyed working across the road from Willi's house. It gave him an easy excuse to see her. This afternoon, she rolled down the window of her rusted car and shouted, "How's it goin' boys?" as if they were kids running into each other. Miles felt the corners of his mouth lift as he talked with her. Afterward Dave had said, "Something going on between you two?" Miles didn't know himself. But for those couple of hours the other night, when Willi fed him and cut his hair, they were a man and a woman who shared something other than a tragedy. He heaved a sigh.

Miles lurched forward as a hand slapped him on the back so hard his chest hit the edge of the Pine Tree's bar.

A man's voice said, "Hey, there, buddy, how you doin'?"

He looked into the face of Junior, who took the stool beside his. Junior's brother Mike sat on the other side, grinning like he'd won big at cards and couldn't wait to tell somebody. Both were high or drunk or both.

Now was the reckoning, and Miles was unsure how to proceed. It didn't matter what he said or did, he was going to get it. Mike was heavier than Miles. He carried the weight of someone who liked booze and greasy food. Junior was short and always trying to make up for it.

Miles put down his bottle. He ran his tongue around the inside of his mouth. He wasn't fooled. Mike's friendly comment was definitely fake. But Junior? Yeah, he, too, but he'd cut him a break.

"I'm sorry, Junior, about what happened to Cody."

Junior fingered the front of Miles's shirt. "You mean hitting him with your truck?"

"That's not the way it happened. I tried to save him."

Junior glanced toward Mike. "That so?"

Miles nodded solemnly, but Junior snorted. "I know what you're thinkin', Miles. I've got brass balls pickin' on you 'cause I didn't give more to that boy or Willi. He was my blood, and I loved his mother when he was born." Junior brought his face closer and gave Miles's shirt a tight twist. "And another thing. I don't want you bothering Willi no more. She's been through enough."

"Get your hands off me, Junior." His voice stayed calm, although his heart had a steady pound. "If you wanna keep this going, let's take it outside. What's it gonna be? The both of you?"

Junior loosened his fingers.

Miles stared at one brother, then the other. When Mike made a snorting laugh, Miles gave him a quick, light shot on the shoulder. Both brothers got to their feet. He stood, too.

"I'm gonna say it again, asshole," Junior said. "Stay away

121

from Willi."

Miles drew his eyes tight. "Don't tell me what to do."

"You'll listen to me if you know what's good for you," Junior said before he and his brother moved to another part of the bar.

Miles drank face forward. He focused on the mirror behind the three shelves of booze. Junior and Mike sat far from the mirror's reach, but by now he didn't care. The two brothers wouldn't be back. They had made their point.

He finished the beer, and although he would have liked another, he fished for a buck in the front pocket of his jeans and flattened it on the bar's top. He made a slow but straight path to the door.

Breaking Snow

Miles drove home, but he wasn't ready to go inside. He glanced at the moonlight, then the snowshoes on the seat beside him. He put a flashlight in the pocket of his down vest and grabbed a cap and gloves. The temperature was in the teens, but he knew breaking snow would get him warm enough to stand it.

This morning when he and Dave stopped on top of the doctor's hill, Miles tried to find the roof to his house. It surprised him how close it was. A snowmobile trail opened midway between his driveway and the Buell Farm. It arced through the lower end of a pasture before it cut through the woods and the back property of the doctor's house. It was a shorter distance than a ride in his truck.

The snow crunched beneath the crampons of his shoes as he followed the side of the road, and then the tracks laid down by the snowmobiles. It was unlikely he'd pass any on his route this time of night, but he'd keep alert for the whine of their engines. No rider would expect a man walking through the woods at night.

A few minutes into it, Miles kept a pace, not as graceful as cross-country skiing, but effective in keeping him above the snow and going forward. His fingers were gorged with blood, so he stuffed his gloves in his pocket. He admired the long, narrow shadows the trees cast upon the snow, the way the moon hung heavy above him, as he shuffled over the trail's rolling landscape until he came near the doctor's house, darkened except for the apartment where Nathan and Martha lived. He turned right along the edge of the road and into Willi's yard. Her small house was lit like a lantern.

Miles stayed in the house's shadow. He saw Willi through a window. She stood, and as he came nearer, he saw her lift a stuffed animal from a cardboard box, then a toy truck. She swiped a sleeve across her face as she sat on a bed. Her head was down and shaking.

He wanted to go inside, say the right things to make her feel better. But what would she think of him walking to her house this late? How would he explain how he felt? So, he kept his watch until she rose and the lights of her house went black one by one.

"Oh, Willi," he said, and feeling cold from stopping, he went back the way he came.

Hard Luck Case

Three days later, Junior was leaving the office of Dexter Propane with his list of stops when he met his father getting out of his wife's car. Pop stuck the end of his cane into the parking lot's dirty snow to pry himself from the car's front seat. He stopped when he saw his oldest son.

"Hey, Pop. How's the bum leg?"

Pop made a low moan in the back of his throat. "Hurts like hell, if you really wanna know. Got a doctor's note sayin' I'll be out another week." He shook his head toward the office window. "The bowlegged bastard's not gonna like that."

Junior's first stop today was an emergency fill in West Hayward, near his mother's house. The family ran out last night. When he told his father, he made a face.

"They're always runnin' out, and sometimes they owe money, so you gotta ask for a check before you can do the delivery. Fuckin' pain in the ass." Pop spat on the snow. "There's a bunch of kids. The husband's never around. At least she's easy to look at."

"Need a hand, Pop?"

At first his father said no, but he gave in, so Junior caught him by the elbow to yank him upright. On the third try, he succeeded.

"Shit, I feel like an old man today."

Junior gave his father a close study. His short whiskers were white, as if the cold had frosted them. He was missing a front tooth and gaining more forehead and gut on his wiry body.

"Aw, you old tomcat, you look fine to me," Junior lied.

Joe cackled as he continued to the office, favoring his good leg.

"Tomcat, you got that right," he said over his shoulder.

Junior drove directly to West Hayward. He thought about

Willi and how he enjoyed helping her with the firewood the other night. He figured she did, too. It was almost like old times, side by side. Her eyes got so wide when he handed her the wad of bills. Better, he figured a way to get Willi the money he owed her. He'd sue Miles Potter. Already, he had called a lawyer who told Junior to set up a time, that he just might have a case. He needed Willi's cooperation, but he had a plan about that.

Junior chuckled. He had already fixed Miles. He got the contractor, a cousin on his mother's side, to lose him the job at the newcomers' house. His cousin was reluctant. He said Miles did high-quality work, the best around for finish carpentry. But blood won out in the end. If Junior had his way, Miles would never work again.

He beeped the truck's horn when he passed his mother's house. Four houses down, he parked the truck in front of the customers' place and went about his work, gripping the nozzle as he hauled the hose through knee-high snow to the empty tank in the backyard. He whistled while it filled. The curtains in one window parted, and two little faces stared at him through the dirty glass. This was a hard luck case. The man was a third-generation drunk, although so far he'd kept a job. Junior gave the kids a wave. He went about what he had to do before he knocked on the door to relight the pilots for the family's water heater and the kitchen range.

The woman answered the door. A baby was on one hip. The little kids had left the window and were huddled behind her. The house was nearly as cold inside as the outside.

"I've got a check for you," she told Junior.

"Thanks, ma'am," he said. "Now, show me what I need to light."

Stirring the Waters

Theresa made Willi do a turn in her new jacket near the front door of the Lucky Lady. She bought it at the outdoor store in Jarvis, not a place she would have normally shopped, but one of her customers told her about a sale, that the jackets were warm and stylish. This one was a royal blue. The man at the counter let her toss her old one in the trash.

"You look great, honey. All the men will be checking you out."

Willi waved her off. "Go on."

Her mother came an hour later for a wash and cut, her second customer this morning. Willi always did her hair at the beauty shop. She'd gladly do it for free at her house, but Ma said it wouldn't feel like the real thing.

Ma settled the nape of her neck into the curved lip of the sink while Willi tested the water's temperature with her hand. She wet her mother's hair, still naturally dark although she was in her fifties. Her mother murmured. She kept her eyes shut while Willi lathered the fruity-smelling shampoo and gave her scalp a scrub with her fingertips.

"Willi, why d'you ask Lorna about the thing you read in the magazine?"

Ma spoke in a voice Willi recognized. Her mother wasn't happy.

"Jesus, Ma, Lorna told you that?"

She lifted her mother's head and swirled her fingers along the back. "Yeah, she did, and it pissed Joe off."

Willi didn't respond as her hands moved over her mother's soapy hair. Now, she understood why her mother was speaking. Joe was mad. It was always Joe first, Lorna second, and then her. Daddy was last. And Cody? Her mother hadn't

127

even asked for his photograph back.

She glanced around the full room. People could hear anything and everything. But even if the place was empty, she'd never tell her mother about Joe. What good would it do? She had decided that sometimes families were like freshwater ponds. As long as no one stirred the muck at the bottom, the water remained clear and blue. For her family, certain topics would do that. Daddy was one. Joe was another. She shook her head. What happened the other day had been a weak attempt on Joe's part, a tasteless joke. The trouble took place years ago.

This family's water, she decided, was best left unstirred.

So instead, Willi concentrated on getting the shampoo out of her mother's hair before she worked in the conditioner. Ma kept her eyes shut except for narrow slits. "Willi, are you listenin' to me?"

"Yeah, I'm listenin', Ma. I don't feel like talkin' about it," she said quietly before pausing. "So, how's Joe's leg? Is he still in pain?"

Her mother hummed. Willi chose the right direction.

"It seems like it's taking longer than the doctor said it would. He can use a cane but pretty much he's laid up in the living room watchin' TV."

Willi toweled her mother's hair. "Come on, Ma. Let's go to my station."

Ma sat in the chair, and as Willi combed her jaw-length hair, she studied their reflections in the mirror. Except for their coloring, they looked like mother and daughter. She parted her mother's hair. Ma hadn't changed her style for years: wavy, with the front smoothed back, except for a few strands across her forehead, so she reminded Willi of that Country and Western singer Patsy Cline. Ma watched Willi in the mirror. Her eyes followed every snip.

"So, Willi, tell me. What does Lorna see in that grease monkey she's dating?"

Willi sighed as she reached for the dryer. "Aw, Ma, Ray's really nice to her. I like him."

"Joe says she could do a lot better than him."

Willi brushed her mother's hair as she worked the dryer, letting its noise cover her words. Ma should be glad Lorna found someone like Ray. She should see his good points. She switched off the dryer and swiveled the chair, so her mother faced the mirror. Willi glanced toward the door as her next customer arrived.

"Gee, Ma, see how pretty you are."

One corner of Ma's mouth twitched upward as she turned her head this way and that. "Not bad," she said.

Willi walked with her mother to her car. Then, she was back at her station, arranging the drape over her next customer, one of her regulars. The woman began telling her a hard-luck story about her ex-boyfriend. They'd been together for three years. She was so sure they'd be getting married, and then he dumped her for her best friend.

But Willi's heart wasn't in the woman's story. She kept thinking about what her mother said. She stayed like that through the morning until a Dexter propane truck pulled in front of the picture window of the Lucky Lady. Its grill came so close to the glass two women gave little shrieks and jumped from beneath the hairdryers.

"Looks like we're getting a delivery today," Theresa said in a deadpan voice over the bleached blonde sitting in her chair.

A man peered into the salon and rapped his knuckles on the glass. The two women moved closer to the window, trying to figure out who he was, but Willi recognized her ex-husband's cowboy hat and mustache. So did the women whose hair was bound up in pink rollers.

"Well, I swear it's Junior Miller," she said.

"Maybe he wants a shave and a haircut, so he stops looking like such a damn redneck," Theresa said, which got the women cackling.

Willi wiped her hands on her apron and excused herself. "I'll see what he wants," she whispered to Theresa.

Junior stayed where he was. His pointed boots smeared what was left of the dirty snow Wayne's shovel threw against the building's front.

"What the hell, Junior. You scared those two women half to

death." Willi's hands were on her hips. "They thought your truck was gonna crash into the place."

"Shit, I'm a better driver than that."

Willi glanced back at the window. The women still stared.

"Why are you here?"

"I wanna ask you to have lunch next door with me."

"Lunch? You want me to have lunch with you?"

Junior made a face. "Yeah. I have somethin' to ask you. Somethin' really important and I can't do it here."

Willi glanced back at the women watching through the window. "I can't. I'm finishing up with a customer right now."

"When you gonna be done? This is really important."

She frowned. "Oh, all right. I can meet you in fifteen minutes."

"Great." Junior grinned. "That's really great Willi. I'll meet you inside."

She hitched a thumb toward the Lucky Lady. "I've gotta go. I've got an old lady under the dryer, and if I don't get back soon, her scalp's gonna burn like bacon."

Fifteen minutes later, Willi walked to the front door of the Chuck Wagon as new snow fell and stuck to the dirty stuff already on the ground. She planned to hear Junior out and then get back to work. It had to be about money, or maybe he was leaving town, which would be a relief. She had enough of the Miller men. In fact, she was thinking of legally changing her name back to Merritt to be clear about her intentions. It was the newest entry on her wish list.

Junior was in a corner booth. He fingered the brim of his black cowboy hat on the tabletop. He had already ordered coffee.

"Well, here I am. What do you want, Junior?"

"Not so fast." He signaled for the waitress, who handed her a menu. "Have whatever you want, Willi. It's on me."

"I'll just have coffee."

"Get more than that. You've gotten awfully skinny, Willi."

The waitress held her pen above the order pad.

"Agnes, I'll have a corn muffin, grilled, please."

Junior's mustache moved when he smiled. "You should've

seen the stop I made this morning. I had to walk in snow up to my hips to reach the tank of this old couple."

"Which old couple?"

"They live out in West Hayward. The old man used to work with your grandfather. Last name's Grissom. Anyway, they were nice about it. They wanted me to come inside to warm up, but the house had that old people smell." He gagged. "I needed to move on 'cause the snow soaked my jeans. Felt like I pissed my pants."

Willi almost laughed.

Junior grinned over his mug of coffee. "How's your car running?

"My car? If you really wanna know, it's got a new noise in the front left wheel, but I made it here, and I'm crossing my fingers I make it home again."

Junior made a face. "Hey, if you get stuck, call me, and I'll give you a lift. I could even lend you my truck so you get to work. You'd just have to drop me off at Dexter and pick me up at the end of the day."

"I dunno, Junior."

"It's no problem. Things are lookin' up. I might be gettin' my own place next month. This job at Dexter is okay, but when the weather breaks this spring, I wanna get back into construction. More money."

Willi frowned. It was as if Junior was moving around and making noise but not going anywhere. She glanced at the wall clock. She had a dye job in twenty minutes.

The waitress placed their orders on the table. Junior got the two-egg special since Chuck served breakfast anytime. He salted his food and whistled as the waitress refilled their cups with coffee. He ate some of the egg and toast.

"Willi, I talked to a lawyer. He says we might have a case against Miles Potter, about how he was responsible for Cody's death."

Something small and sharp buzzed inside Willi. "What are you talkin' about?"

"The lawyer says maybe we can prove Miles was at fault. Like he saw Cody comin' down the hill before it happened, but

131

he didn't do nothin' about it. The lawyer wants to meet you next week to get your side of the story. We don't have a case unless you're part of it."

"You're joking. Right?"

"Course not. If you're worried about the money, the lawyer doesn't get a cent unless he wins, and then he gets a third."

She cringed as his hand brushed hers. "Junior, why you doin' this?"

"Why? 'Cause I want you to have the money. It's no skin off Miles Potter's nose. His insurance company will pay."

"No, I want nothin' to do with a lawsuit. Leave Miles alone. You don't know what happened. You weren't there." Her voice rose. "You were off somewhere in New Hampshire having a fun time as usual. You didn't care about Cody. That's his name, by the way."

Junior's head moved in quick, little shakes. "I know his name's Cody. I'm the one who picked it. Remember? And I know I was a shitty father. Let me fix somethin' for once."

"No."

His eyes went side to side as he played with his mustache. "Just think it over."

"Junior, I don't want a thing from you. Forget you owe me anything. Forget you even knew me."

Willi stood so fast the dishes clattered on the table, and Junior didn't have time to make a rebuttal, although his mouth hung open while she left.

The Upward Slant

Miles held the drill steady as the bit shot upward through the maple's bark. The tree, about a foot around, could take two taps. For a tree in a well-used sugar bush, Miles would have to drill a hole about six inches from the one done last year. But it's been decades since the maples on the doctor's hill had been tapped. It likely happened when men hung buckets on metal spigots and used oxen to tow a wagon holding wooden barrels filled with sap back to the sugarhouse.

A few yards behind, Shane Buell, the youngest of his neighbors' eight children, hammered the plastic taps attached to the tubing into the holes. The kid was fourteen and had a hand for the job, his aim not so hard he'd break the tap, but enough so it stayed in place. Miles tried to keep ahead of the boy by a few trees.

Shane took after most of his brothers, dark and with one eyebrow. Black whiskers grew in long strands, like shreds of wire over his upper lip. The pimples on his forehead and chin resembled drops of jelly.

"You okay back there?" Miles called.

The kid said "Yup," which was his typical answer to most questions Miles posed since they had arrived this morning. Miles was used to Dave's outgoing nature, his running commentary about his family, the town, and politics. It didn't matter the subject. He often knew enough to speak on it. In that regard, Dave reminded Miles of Linwood.

Now in the silence, Miles's mind wandered to his situation. Last night, he spoke with his mother, who said she and his father were planning to be back this spring. They missed Hayward. She asked about the weather and the health of her friends. Was he keeping busy with work?

"Mom, I've been working with Dave, getting him ready for sugaring," he had told her. "It's a little slow right now, but work should pick up when the weather breaks."

He didn't want to dwell on his problems with his mother. She used to say when he was a boy he had to apply himself, as if she were talking to the parents of one of her students. But her words didn't leave an impression on him. He got by in high school, didn't in college. He let relationships with women slip from him. The only thing he stuck with has been carpentry, and only because Linwood coaxed him to stay until he realized working with wood was something he liked and did well.

For the past few days, he and Dave fixed lines of tubing on Lawson's Hill and the small sugar bush behind his house. Dave left the lines in place at the end of last season, although he pulled the taps from the trees and flushed them clean. Today, he and Shane were back tapping the doctor's sugar bush, while Dave and another Buell worked elsewhere. The boys were available since they were on school vacation this week.

The drill buzzed in Miles's hand while he pondered how Shane and Kevin Buell would likely never live anywhere but Hayward. If they did, it'd be one of the neighboring towns. For poor families like the Buells, who lived in Hayward as long as the Potters, the town's roads seemed to slant so hard toward the center, it took too much effort to leave. Shane and Kevin were farm kids. They showed their cows at the 4-H fair, and Shane, when pressed, could answer any of Miles's questions about livestock.

"Hey, Shane, what are you planning to do when you get out of high school?"

Shane glanced up from the tap in his hand. His brow creased in the center as he held his hammer mid-air.

"Work the farm with Pop," Shane said directly, as if it were the most obvious answer.

Miles nodded and lifted his snowshoes to the next tree. Snow caked the legs of his jeans.

"Well, it looks as if we'll be neighbors for a long time," he said.

The boy made a laugh high in his throat.

Wet flakes as big as blossoms fell in a late winter snow. He and Shane only worked in their flannel shirts and vests because the exertion of moving on snowshoes kept them warm. They were halfway up the doctor's hill, making excellent progress. Dave, who kept a close eye on the weather forecast, predicted the sap would begin running within a week. He showed Miles where the snow's height had diminished as the ground melted it from beneath. Miles knew what that meant. Soon, there would be afternoons of shuttling sap back to the sugarhouse. He'd work the evaporator with Dave, stoking the fire with chunks of slab wood, so the sap in its pan held a boil. They'd stay up nights, fueled by coffee, conversation, and Ruth's food.

A car horn beeped steadily below. It belonged to the pickup truck Shane's mother drove. She kept sounding the horn. Shane told Miles he'd better get down the hill fast, his longest sentence since Miles asked whether cows minded the snow.

"Nah, but they can't stand a cold rain," Shane answered that one.

Miles knew this morning he'd be losing his helper in the late afternoon. He stood tall to stretch his back. "I'll manage without you. Just leave the snowshoes in the cab of my truck. See you tomorrow."

The boy left with a grunt.

Miles worked on a strategy. He would drill five trees, then go back to hammer the taps. He might be better off quitting with the boy, but he relished seeing the view from the top of the hill as his reward. Tomorrow they'd follow another system of lines up the hill.

He turned backward, almost losing his balance, when he heard the crunch of snow. Perhaps Shane's mother had relented, but Miles caught a flash of blue ascending the hill. He grinned when he recognized Willi. Snowflakes melted as they touched her hair. She stopped in her snowshoes when she was a few feet from Miles. A shy smile was on her face.

"This is a nice surprise," he said.

She lifted one of the snowshoes she wore a few inches.

"I grabbed these off Shane." Her voice was breathy from the climb. "They worked well when I was going uphill. Didn't slide once."

She had pulled her hair back in one braid that started at the crown of her head, but it was loosening so strands hung softly around her face. Her chest rose and fell. Miles felt like placing a hand there to feel its rhythm. But he resisted.

"Now that you're here, maybe I should put you to work," he said.

Her face held onto her smile. "Why not? I got nothin' better to do. I got off work early 'cause the Lucky Lady lost water. Somethin's wrong with the line from the well. Theresa was chewin' out Wayne when I left."

Miles murmured when he realized she'd be staying.

"I'll let you do the hammering. Let me show you how." He hit the tap into the hole. "Pretty easy, eh? Here's the hammer. Why don't you try?"

Willi's first shot was tentative, but she set the tap on the second.

"That's good, Willi. Maybe, I'll turn you into a carpenter."

For the next half hour, they worked together drilling and tapping. Like him, she didn't wear gloves. She kept humming in a voice high and sweet. He tried to recognize the tune but ended up asking.

"Oh, it's something from Jimmie Rogers. Pa loved to pick his tunes."

They took a break three-quarters of the way up the hill.

"Willi, guess what I saw today? The blade of a scythe stuck in a tree. Someone must've leaned the tool against the trunk, and it grew around the blade. You couldn't remove it without killing the tree." He rubbed his hands together. "There must be a lesson there somewhere."

"Uh-huh, don't be so careless with your tools," she said.

He laughed with her.

By the time they reached the top of the hill, the advancing storm hastened dusk. They put on their gloves and brushed snow from a short outcropping of ledge for a seat. Already a couple of inches had fallen. From what he saw, the roads were only wet, but if this snow kept up that would change. Miles pointed here and there to give Willi her bearings.

"Oh, there's my house." Her voice withered. "It's not much of anything, is it?"

"I don't know about that. It wouldn't take much to fix it up. And it sits on a real pretty piece of land. Your grandfather gave it to you, right?"

Willi nodded. "He did. I was surprised when I found out, but then Pa was awfully kind to Cody and me. So was his brother, Boyd. I told you about him."

"Uh-huh. I remember him," Miles said. "He ran the auction barn in the southern part of town."

"I used to drive Pa there on Sundays. He and Uncle Boyd and some of their buddies got together to make music and drink sippin' whiskey. I sat in the back while Cody played with the things Uncle Boyd had for sale. Those old guys were fun to listen to. They'd joke about what they did when they were boys, the hell they raised in Hayward, gettin' drunk, racing their junks, and climbing each other's roofs. Those were fun times listening to 'em."

He and Willi may have grown up together, but she lived in a different kind of town, a rougher place where families suffered long from the mistakes a few of their people made. For Willi, that meant her father died in a car crash, leaving her mother with nothing to raise her girls. If Miles's father had died, his mother wouldn't have worried. The house didn't have a mortgage. He had life insurance. There was money in the bank, lots of it.

Miles showed her the roof of his house and how it could be reached by snowmobile.

"Uh-huh. Junior came that way to see me one time," she said.

"Junior?"

She frowned.

"Uh-huh. He's been to see me a few times. He thinks he can fix everything he broke. But it doesn't work that way. I don't mind him paying the money he owes, but that's it between us as far as I'm concerned." She was quiet for a while. "He wants to make big trouble for you, Miles. He says he talked to a lawyer."

"Because of the accident? I'm not surprised." He stared at the snowy ground, then Willi's face. "Tell me, Willi. How do you feel about all of this? Honestly."

Her red woolen gloves gripped each other.

"I told Junior I'm not goin' along with it. I was there. I know what really happened that day. Believe me. I think about it all the time."

"Willi, you don't have to talk about this," he said.

She shook her head.

"It's all right. Let me say it." She swallowed. "I was hanging wet clothes and it was almost dark. I gave Cody a ride in his sled. He was hollerin' and makin' such a fuss 'cause he wanted another. He was on his belly, using his mittens to push himself around. I shouldn't have let him do that. I should've stopped what I was doin' and taken him in the house. But I didn't. I kept hanging those stupid clothes." Her words kept breaking. "Then, outta the corner of my eye, I saw him go. I ran but couldn't catch him. His sled went so fast over that snow, and I kept falling through. And then, I saw you with him at the bottom of the hill. Oh, Miles, that's what really happened."

Miles put his arm around Willi. Her body trembled beneath her thick coat.

"I'm so sorry, Willi."

"It's *my* fault he died. *All my fault*. Not yours."

"It was an accident, Willi. You didn't want it to happen." His voice was soft. "You loved your little boy. You were just alone, and it was really hard."

She raised her chin. Tears were smeared across her face. He moved closer. So sad. So beautiful. He kissed her wet cheek, and then her lips. He kissed her again, and afterward neither spoke as the storm settled heavy flakes upon the hill. The corners of her mouth quivered upward as he brushed snow from her hair.

"Willi, this snow isn't going to stop anytime soon. I think we'd better get going, don't you?"

"Could you stay this time?"

"You sure, Willi?"

"I'm sure."

He kissed her quickly and bent to gather the tools. "Stay close behind," he told her.

They began their descent. Miles led the way, whistling, slowing his pace for her since the fresh snow was slippery. Willi watched her feet as she walked. At the bottom, she handed him the snowshoes and pushed her boots into the snow collected on the road. She went ahead to unchain her dog, and Miles drove his truck up the driveway, following the blue of her jacket through the snowfall.

Good Again

Miles kissed Willi as he danced her backward into her bedroom. They tumbled onto her bed, stripping off their clothes and touching each other. She was all breath and whimpers, moving beneath him and calling his name.

It all felt good.

Later, he woke first. The wind drove the snow sideways against her house. But her body warmed him.

The kerosene lamp on her dresser was lit. He raised the sheet to study her shapes and shadows. Her belly had a small scar, and Willi slid his fingers away when he touched the rough sliver of skin. Her eyes were half-open.

"The doctors cut me there when Cody was born," she said.

She smiled with closed lips when he covered the scar with the palm of his hand, then kissed her mouth. The windows rattled in their sash. She waited for what he would do next.

Keeping Up

Junior just finished supper and his third beer at the Pine Tree Tavern when one of the town's road crew stopped to fill a thermos with coffee. The driver tipped his head toward the idling truck parked outside the front windows. He said the men couldn't keep up with the storm, so the road boss ordered them to give up on the back ways for now. The fire station was ready to take in anyone who got stranded.

The driver spoke in a quick, high voice. "They're talkin' on the radio about a foot and a half of snow tonight. Do you believe it?"

Junior pulled at the hairs of his mustache as he listened to the man. He didn't want to get stuck at his mother's in the town's west end, so he couldn't make it to work on time tomorrow. He needed the job and the money. For the same reason, he rejected the waitress's offer to stay at her place because her driveway was long and steep.

"Some other night, sweetheart," he said as he rose to call his mother.

Mom answered on the sixth ring. Junior visualized her sitting in her robe as she soaked her feet in a tub of hot water. The cat would be on her lap, so she'd have to work to reach the phone on the end table.

"Hey, it's me, Junior. It's snowing like a son of a gun, and the roads are bad, so I'm gonna stay at Pop's tonight. You gonna be all right alone?"

"Don't you worry about me. I'm stayin' put. I'm used to being by myself."

"Right, Mom."

Junior made a call to Pop, who told him to come over. He had one more beer before he split the Pine Tree, where a few diehards kept drinking and watching the weather report on the TV set behind the bar. The truck's rear swayed as Junior drove the few miles to the town's main village where his father and his wife lived. He slowed and backed the pickup into the driveway next to Lorna's car. He figured he'd just shovel his way out in the morning. Besides, Lorna would be up before him, and she'd end up doing most of the work, which seemed like a good plan.

He dumped his boots next to the kitchen door and said hello to Lorna, who shuffled a deck of cards at the table. Her mother already had gone to bed, so she and Pop played cards to pass the time, although right now, Lorna explained, he was using the toilet.

"What are you two playin'? Strip poker?"

Lorna shot him a deadly look as she moved the cards up and down in the palm of her hand.

"You're sick, Junior, real sick."

He forced a laugh.

"You're right, Lorna. Why don't you and me play strip poker instead?"

Another time Lorna would have come back with a smart remark but not tonight. Instead, she slammed the deck on the Formica tabletop. She snapped her lighter as she jammed a butt in her mouth. She blew smoke in his face.

"Like I said, real sick."

Junior stretched his legs over the linoleum floor, conscious of the holes in the soles of each sock, but he didn't care. He knew Lorna wouldn't. He might like playing strip poker with her and finally getting a peek at those big tits of hers. Ray was probably one satisfied guy rolling around with a woman like her. But Junior already had bad luck with one Merritt sister. He wasn't going to try another, especially one as moody as Lorna.

"Take it easy, Lorna. I was only kiddin' you. Can't you take a joke no more?"

"Shut up, Junior."

"Now, tell me, did I just see a smile on that face of yours?"

The toilet in the bathroom next to the kitchen flushed twice. Pop leaned heavily on his cane after he shut the door behind him. He gave Junior a nod as he hobbled to his chair. It didn't appear he was going back to work anytime soon.

"I'd stay out of there if I were you. I stunk up the place," Pop announced.

"What else is new?" Lorna said.

Pop twisted his lips in an ornery scowl. "You got a fresh mouth, Lorna. Just like your Ma."

"Sorry, Dad," Lorna said.

The three of them sat around the table, drinking beer and talking.

Junior cleared his throat.

"I talked to Willi the other day," he said. "I told her about the lawyer, but she won't have nothin' to do with it. You should've heard her stick up for the guy."

Pop formed his mouth as if it were holding something sour.

"There's somethin' wrong inside that little girl's head," he said. "She's shown no gratitude to this family since day one. The only ones she cared about were her father and grandfather. The old man I could understand. He put a roof over her head. But her father was a loser. You should hear Marjorie talk about how he'd get drunk and cry like a baby. What kinda man does that?"

"He was my daddy, too," Lorna said quietly.

Pop cleared his throat and frowned. "Sorry, honey, I didn't mean to bad-mouth your dad. It's just your sister makes me so mad sometimes."

Junior tried to remember when his father ever said anything nice about Willi, and he came up empty. When he told Pop he wanted to marry Willi, he said, "What d'you do? Knock her up? Nah? So, what are you gonna do that for? Keep screwin' her, boy, but don't marry her."

Lorna rose, reminding them she had to get up early for her job at the bakery. But Junior heard her make a call on the living room phone. It was probably to that boyfriend of hers because her voice played up and down in the other room.

Pop sucked his snot. "Shit, she's gone cuckoo over that grease ball. Let's hope she don't get knocked up, and we've got a bunch of retards hanging around the house."

Junior winced.

Pop reached inside the refrigerator for two more cans of beer. He tossed one to Junior before he hoisted himself upright with his cane. He complained about his ankle the whole way to the couch in the living room, where he plopped himself into a reclining position. Lorna had already left. Junior took an easy chair as his father grabbed the TV's remote control from the coffee table. He craned his head toward Junior.

"Wait'll you see what's on this channel, boy."

A movie was in progress. A guy was getting it on with two women, something he, and he guessed his father, had never done. The women had breasts as big as udders and blonde hair. They let the man watch them kiss and play with each other before they turned on him. Now, Junior wished he had gone home with the waitress, long driveway or not.

The TV's picture went fuzzy. Pop cursed about the snow and banged on the floor with the tip of his cane. "Junior, go outside and clear off the satellite dish, will you? Shit, we're missin' the best parts."

Without saying a word, Junior went to the kitchen to get his boots. His father's house was so overheated, he welcomed the walk outside. The air, just cold enough to permit snow, revived him. Flakes clung to the shoulders of his shirt as he marched to the backyard, using the lights from the house as a guide. He found the satellite dish and swiped it clear with the side of his hand, although he figured if the snow kept up, he'd be back out here again.

His father was one happy guy when Junior found him on the couch. Pop pointed to the screen where the man was slapping the bare ass of a woman. Junior resumed his spot in the easy chair.

"Knew you was useful for somethin', boy."

Junior stayed up until midnight. He slept on a single bed in Willi's old room on the second floor. The place was as sterile as a motel room off a small state highway. Nothing of hers was left. He lay in bed thinking about how he blew that thing with the lawyer. He should've known better to rush Willi. It took him months to convince her to marry him. The first time he asked, they were naked on his bed, and he felt he couldn't possibly be happier. All things seemed possible at that moment: a home, kids, maybe his own excavation business.

He didn't expect her answer.

"I dunno, Junior," she said. "You think it'd be the right thing to do?"

Junior had studied her face. Willi didn't think their relationship would last. Nothing in her life had so far.

"Prove it to me," she said that night, and he remembered sadly the chance she gave him.

So Damn Hard

The next morning, Junior felt smug because his propane truck was one of the few vehicles on the road. The roads had been cleared, but yesterday's storm sealed most people's driveways with deep, wet banks that would remain that way until a plow truck cleared them.

His boss was pleased to see his prompt arrival this morning. He told him to deliver propane to the senior housing first, but Junior had another idea. He'd go directly to the doctor's house on Willi's hill, which would give him an excuse to check on her. It was Willi's day off, her mother told him this morning over coffee, so he'd stop to show he cared. He wouldn't talk about suing Miles Potter unless she did.

Junior turned left onto Barker Road, and despite the snow, the truck took the hill easily. Willi's ratty little mutt stood guard on the snowbank at the top of the driveway, yipping at his truck. Junior chuckled. "Come on, try to catch me, you little bitch."

A tractor was clearing snow from Willi's driveway. Her mother said Nathan plowed it for free after he finished his work at the doctor's farm. The man had a neighborly heart Junior could appreciate.

Junior whistled as he continued up Barker Road until he reached the doctor's driveway and turned around. But he swore when he saw Willi standing in her nightgown in the door with Miles Potter. His pickup was buried in snow. The two of them turned when they heard the engine of his truck, and Junior felt low when Willi's smile faded.

Junior saw her in his mirror. She gazed up at Miles as they talked. He was ready to stop the truck, but he kept going. Willi was making it so damn hard for him.

A Pretty Picture

Later that afternoon, Nathan used the bucket of his tractor to clear a space large enough off the road for the five-hundred-gallon plastic vat on the bed of Dave's truck. Snow clung to the trees, but it was warming, so gobs of it shed below. Willi stood near Miles and the two Buell boys, who silently appraised Nathan's slow progress. The brothers smoked roll-your-owns and watched what Dave was doing. The fresh snow only went a foot or so, but the rest was solid.

"Dave should've cleared this out earlier in the winter, then kept at it," Shane Buell told his brother. "That's the way our dad would have done it."

The tractor was back on the road, Nathan's part in this job was done, and he sat aloft as Dave backed his one-and-a-half-ton truck closer to the spot. One of the Buell boys leaped onto its bed and helped Miles and his brother slide the plastic vat forward. They tipped it onto the clearing and worked at making it level.

"Good enough for me. What do you think, boys?" Miles asked.

The Buells nodded.

A car sounded its horn. Willi stepped aside for the doctor's Volvo, which stopped ahead of the tractor. For several moments, the doctor stood near the open door of his car.

"I'm not sure, Dave, if that's the right spot." He rubbed his smooth, pink chin. "What about over there? That way you won't see it easily from the road."

Dave got out of the driver's seat.

"This is really the only place for it because of the ledge on this hill." He reached for the stack of gray metal buckets in the truck's cab. He put a cover on one and held it up for the doctor. "When I put these up, oh, about two to a tree, your eyes won't even notice the white, plastic vat. You and your friends will see a line of buckets going up to your house on both sides of the road. It'll make a pretty picture, don't you think?"

The doctor squinted at the row of trees. "Yes, I can see that."

Dave smiled. "I'm expecting the sap will make its first run tomorrow or the next day. I'll be at my sugarhouse boiling at night. Maybe you'd like to give Miles and me a hand. It's hard, hot work, but you might enjoy it. Right, Miles?"

"Yup, you haven't lived up here until you can say you spent a night keeping the fire hot enough for a good boil," he said.

Willi admired Dave for the way he handled the doctor, who didn't have enough manners to say hello first to any of them. His words must have worked because the doctor nodded as if a spring were in his neck. He bought the scene all right.

"I might like to try that," the doctor said before he glanced around him. "Oh, hello."

Willi and the doctor were only neighbors by location. She bet her little shack spoiled his country postcard. If she had the money, she'd ask Miles to fix it nice. But she had more pressing worries than that. Ray said her car wouldn't pass inspection this spring. He showed her the bottom was so rusted a heavy man's foot could push through to the pavement. It was only one of its serious problems.

"This car is ready to fall apart around you," Ray said. "It's not safe. I wouldn't drive too far if I was you and hope you don't have an accident."

She watched Miles have an easy time with the Buell brothers. The good feeling from last night didn't end, even after Junior drove by her house this morning. Miles told her not to worry. He'd handle everything. Now, he laughed as he slapped one of the brothers on the back.

"I don't know how we managed without the doctor's help," Miles joked.

The boys made little snorting laughs. She laughed with them.

Willi's ears caught the sound of a familiar car engine

148

straining up the hill. It was Lorna's big Ford, and when her sister stopped, she rolled down her window. The features on her face had an unpleasant twist. "Aw, shit, Willi, don't tell me you forgot."

She and Lorna were supposed to shop today for a birthday present for their mother. They knew exactly what they wanted to get her. Ma collected decorated plates, they covered a wall in her living room, but she coveted one she saw in a gift shop in Jarvis. Ma wanted one called "Jailhouse Rock" with Elvis dressed in black, his hips cocked, a bad-boy expression on his face. Ma went to the store twice but didn't buy it because it was so expensive. Willi and Lorna planned to go halves.

Willi glanced over the hood of the car at Miles, then her sister.

"No, Lorna, I didn't forget," she lied. "Why don't you go to the house? I have to get my bag and put Foxy inside."

"Hurry up, Willi," Lorna complained. "You should've been ready already."

Willi waited until her sister's car was gliding up the driveway before she told Miles she had to go. He held his face near hers. "I can see you later tonight. Right?"

"I dunno when we'll be back, but the door's never locked. You can wait for me there."

The Buell boys snickered.

"Hey, knock it off, you two," Miles said over his shoulder. He turned toward Willi. "Don't mind them."

The Buells were not Willi's biggest concern. Lorna stood beside her car at the bottom of the driveway. She was squinting hard. Willi wondered what she'd tell her sister.

Jailhouse Rock

Willi and Lorna didn't speak during the first half of the trip to Irma's Attic. Lorna chain-smoked with the window down and drove close to the car up ahead.

"Jesus, Lorna, take it easy, will you? We'll get there before it closes."

Lorna tossed her lit butt out the window and eased up on the gas. She gave her sister a menacing stare. "I saw that fuck-me-please look you gave him."

"Huh?"

"Don't give me that."

Willi felt her face go red. "I-I-I dunno what you're talkin' about."

"Yeah, you do, and I bet my ass you've already done it. Jesus, Willi, what would Ma say if she knew?"

Willi was quiet. Lorna sounded just like Ma. Both didn't like being around people who owned more because it made them feel they had less.

"The nut don't fall far from the tree," Ma used to say whenever Willi said something nice about Miles when they were kids. She pushed the end of her nose upward with the tip of her finger, so it formed a pig's snout. "So don't you be gettin' any ideas. He's not our kind."

But unlike Ma, Willi could reach her sister. They've always been close, especially after Daddy died. They learned to play silently, so they didn't bother their mother, who seemed more angry than sad after Daddy had died.

"Lorna, I don't care what Ma thinks about Miles. What do you think she says about Ray? Please, be on my side this time."

Lorna slowed her car as they approached the gift shop's

150

parking lot. She gave Willi a sideways glance. "All right, you win. But I'll knock his head off if he hurts you."

"Lorna, you don't mean that."

"Yeah, I do." She grabbed her bag from the back seat. "Let's get inside before the store closes. Hey, why don't we go to the Pine Tree for burgers and beer after we're done? Yeah? But I'm cutting you off at two beers. No crybaby stuff this time."

Willi smiled at her sister. "I dunno what you're talkin' about."

The tables and glass cases inside Irma's Attic were jammed with figurines, stuffed animals, and trinkets, but Willi and Lorna bypassed them for the wall of plates. There were hundreds of them. Irma, a short, round woman, raved about her selection.

"Best in the county, maybe the state," she said.

"We only came for Elvis," Lorna interrupted her.

The woman's eyes shined as she called them to the far left, where Elvis posed on several porcelain plates. It was the young Elvis before he got fat and full of drugs. He was still swiveling his hips. No wonder Ma liked him.

Lorna pointed toward one on the top row. "There it is. The 'Jailhouse Rock' plate. It's the one Ma wants."

"I dunno. I kinda like the 'Suspicious Minds' plate better," Willi said. "Elvis is making a face like he doesn't trust anybody. That's more like Ma, don't you think?"

Irma's mouth hung open, but Lorna slapped Willi's arm and guffawed. They were happy sisters again, plotting against their mother. "Don't mind my sister," Lorna told the woman. "She's got a weird sense of humor."

"I see," the woman said as she reached for the plate.

151

Sister Fun

Miles was waiting in Willi's house when she and Lorna returned. He started a fire, and the dog slept on the couch beside him. Willi whistled for Foxy to get down, but she didn't listen. Miles laughed.

"You're such a bad dog," Willi said.

Lorna gave Miles the evil eye. "I just came in to make sure it was safe for my sister. You can never be too careful these days. Right, Miles?"

Willi set the gift box on the kitchen table and raised the plate to show Miles. Her eyes were big and playful as she tilted her head to the side.

"This is for Ma. What do you think, Miles?"

Miles chuckled. "Well, if it isn't the King himself. Your mother's an Elvis fan?"

"Big time," Lorna said. "Once when she was a girl at the Penfield Fair, she paid five dollars she saved from her babysitting money, so she could sit in the back seat of Elvis's old pink Cadillac someone had and was showing it off around the country. Ma said she felt like Elvis' girlfriend sitting there."

"It sounds like you made the right choice for a gift," Miles told her.

Lorna beamed and elbowed her sister playfully. "Maybe he's all right."

Willi elbowed her back. Miles glanced from one sister to another as if he were waiting for the punch line.

"Just sister fun," Willi told him.

The First Run

Sap flowed into the metal holding tank at the sugarhouse, sweet music to Dave, who threw up his arms and did a jig next to the evaporator. "I knew it, I knew it," he sang. "I just knew it."

Dave's little girls danced with him, although they didn't understand what their father was shouting about.

His wife, Ruth, whose belly was too big to dance, laughed and shook her head. "You gotta love the man," she said.

Miles laughed as he stoked the fire beneath the evaporator's pan. He was doing as Dave taught him, putting the slabs of hard and soft wood, bark-side down, in the firebox. His goal was to get its cast-iron doors hot enough to glow red. Now the firebox's ears, or hinges, were another thing. Dave, who learned to sugar from an old-timer long dead, said he only did it once so far.

Miles stripped to his thermal shirt. He couldn't work bare-shirted because sparks flaring from the firebox's opening would burn his skin. The shirt and jeans would be useless by the end of sugaring season, bit through with so many holes they'd look like someone had fired birdshot at him. Miles reached inside his jeans pockets for the coins and keys. He took off his belt. He had learned from Dave their metal would heat up enough to leave red marks on his body.

"Hey, Dave, you might want to forget to tell the doctor about emptying his pockets when he comes for his ceremonial boil. We'd get a laugh watching him jump around like his pants were on fire."

"Yeah, that'd go over big," Dave said flatly.

Yesterday, when the temperature rose into the forties and everyone's houses dripped melted snow, some sap collected in the vats at the bottom of each sugar bush. Today, the run was full-blown with two thousand gallons ready to be boiled into syrup.

Dave was full of local lore as he moved around the sugarhouse after Ruth and the girls went home. He talked about how farmers in New England used to make maple sugar, forming it into hard cakes. Maple syrup became popular in the late 1800s when someone invented the evaporator, which resembles a flat-bottom boat when it's empty.

Miles glanced up from the firebox's door. He raised a gloved hand.

"Dave, you've told me this story six years straight. Why don't you tell me this on the third week when we're so sick of this stuff and pulling all-nighters we vow never to do it again? Or better yet, save it for the doctor. I bet he'd love telling his buddies back in New York all about it."

Dave studied Miles.

"Shit, you can be such a spoilsport sometimes." He reached for his leather gloves. "Anyway, around the Civil War people up North began using maple sugar instead of cane sugar and molasses from the South. They used to call it northern comfort."

"Yeah, yeah, I remember that from last year."

The sugarhouse, only yards from Dave's house, was unheated, except for the evaporator's fire box. Step a few feet outside at night, and the cold had a punch, but next to the evaporator, all was humid and hot like a woman's mouth. The swirling sap in the pan gave off a bank of steam, which rose to the sugarhouse's vented roof.

They fired up the evaporator about an hour ago. It'd be another two before Dave could pour the season's first syrup. As Dave reminded Miles, the first boil sweetens the pan, so it takes longer than the next firings. They'd be here until ten or so and resume boiling the next day.

Miles helped Dave build his sugarhouse seven years ago. They took measurements from an abandoned shack in South Hayward that had collapsed from heavy snow the year before Dave's was built. Rough-hewn boards nailed vertically covered the rectangular building. On the wall near the shelf for the radio, Dave penciled the starting and ending dates for each season, and how many gallons of syrup they had made. Today's date was Thursday, March 5.

154

"Where's Willi?" Dave shouted over the radio's oldies station.

"She should be coming later."

"Seems like you two are getting pretty close."

"Close? I hope so."

Since their first night, Miles only went home to change his clothes. He turned his furnace on low and didn't care what spoiled in his refrigerator. He only wanted to be with Willi and thought about her when he wasn't.

Miles popped open the fire box's doors with the butt end of a log. He shoved slab wood inside, where the coals inside were an unholy red.

"Ruth and I were talking about her the other night," Dave said. "We remembered the last time her grandfather and his brother, Boyd, played at Town Hall."

"When was that?"

"It must've been a couple of years before her grandfather died. Town Hall was packed, but we lucked out with seats toward the front." Dave began chuckling. "Willi walked her grandfather up the center aisle. The old man wore a straw cowboy hat and a bolo tie. She treated her grandfather like he was king of the Grand Ole Opry." He shook his head. "Old Pete was so damned proud to be beside her."

"That so."

"Yup, old Pete Merritt gripped Willi's right hand as she held the handle of his guitar case with the other. Her boy, Cody, just a little thing then, was right behind her, clutching the back hem of her skirt. Willi helped her grandfather up the steps of the stage to his seat and bent to remove his guitar from the case. She kissed her grandfather's forehead. The man beamed like sunshine and patted Cody's head. She brought the boy to the front row where he sat in her lap the entire time.

"He dedicated the first song to Willi. It was something he wrote. I think he called it 'My Sweet Girl' or something like that. Were you there?" Dave blew a sharp whistle. "No? Too bad."

Miles fed the firebox as he tried to remember where he'd been and thought that might have been the night his father had

155

his stroke. He and his mother spent most of it in the hospital, waiting to see how things would turn out.

"I'm sure sorry I missed it," he said as he shut the iron doors.

Signs

The firebox's doors glowed red when Miles heard the rattling engine of Willi's car. He called to Dave, who stacked slab wood in the adjoining shed. He tossed his gloves to Dave. "Hey, I have to go outside for a minute. Could you mind the fire?"

Miles grinned when he saw Willi walk through the dark toward the sugar shack. He hurried toward her. "Hey, watch your step there."

She giggled as she reached up to ruffle his hair.

"Nice haircut."

"Yeah, it is."

Miles showed Willi where to put her things as he took over for Dave, who needed to check the pump sucking sap from the truck's vat. It was a job he would give to the Buell kids, who would help once the season got going. The Buells liked all things mechanical and preferred running machinery to the grunt work of feeding a stove, although they did it without complaint if Dave asked.

Willi sat on the wooden bench jammed in a corner. Her eyes shined. "I smelled my first skunk this morning on the way to work," she said. "That's a sure sign of spring."

Miles grinned.

"Yeah, that's one," he said. "You ready for your mother's party?"

Willi's reply was interrupted by voices at the door as Ruth and the two girls, dressed in nightgowns beneath their winter coats, came inside the shack. Willi smiled when Ruth, who smoothed her hands over her large belly, greeted her.

"Haven't seen you in a long time," Ruth said, as she introduced her two girls, Emma and Nell.

Emma, the older, twirled her red hair in her fingers. "Willi? That's a boy's name."

"Yeah, some people have said that." She squinted at Miles. "My real name's Wilhelmina, after my grandma, but no one *ever* calls me that."

Miles warned the girls to keep back as he swung open the doors to load more wood into the firebox. He let Dave test and pour the finished syrup into the jugs. His job was to keep the fire going. He didn't mind the repetitive work of moving wood from the shed to its oblivion inside the firebox. Sometimes Miles's brain was numbed nicely by the routine, but most of the time he let it ramble. Tonight, before Willi came, he was thinking about his mother, who called to report on his father's declining health, how he didn't seem interested in much these days. Miles told her the trees' tender branches have reddened and the cover of snow was shrinking fast. He bet the pussy willows would sprout soon in the drainage ditch in front of their home.

Willi chatted with Dave's girls as her long fingers wove Emma's hair into a braid. She used her own barrette to hold the end in place, and as Willi's blond hair fell loosely around her neck, a hum escaped his mouth. Ruth gave Miles an amused look, and he bent his head to finish the load.

Fine Things

Later, after he and Dave finished the first batch of syrup, Willi went with Miles to his parents' house. His mother asked twice that he check on the house, and he knew better than to chance a third. Willi left her car at Dave's. They'd stop back later for it.

Inside, they walked through the still, warm rooms. Miles flicked lights on and off as he checked each one. Nothing was amiss.

"Your parents have nice things. Look at all those books."

"You've never been here before?"

She shook her head no, and then he recalled when they were kids, she was never invited to his house even for birthday parties. He sighed. The other night when he and his mother spoke, he mentioned he was seeing a lot of Willi.

His mother was silent for a moment before she said, "That's very thoughtful of you, Miles. Helping her out like that after all she's been through. Poor girl."

"It's not like that, Mom," he said, and she went "Oh."

It'll take time to win her over.

In the living room, Willi stopped before a small end table. She bent to examine the legs. She stood, grinning. "I bet your mother bought this at Uncle Boyd's."

"Mom was always buying things there. How do you know?"

"It used to be mine."

"What? You sure?"

"Uh-huh. See this mark? Cody made that with one of his toys."

She sat on the couch, an antique his mother paid a woman in town to reupholster with a burgundy velvet. Miles sat beside her. "If you want, I could ask my mother to give it back," he said.

Willi shook her head.

"It doesn't mean that much to me," she said, sighing. "I got pretty desperate for money after Junior stopped paying me child support. So, I called Uncle Boyd to come see the furniture and stuff I had. My Great-Aunt Regina gave 'em to me when she retired to Florida. I asked Uncle Boyd if there's anything worth selling."

"Uncle Boyd told me, 'Well, Willi, I don't see any treasures, but I think I can find buyers for most of your things, if that's what you want.' Then he said, 'Does my brother know you're doin' this?' I told him not to tell Pa."

Her voice fell to a whisper. Miles glanced around at the fine things in this house, and then the little table. How much did his mother spend for it?

"I'd call up Uncle Boyd, and he'd take whatever I asked him to." She stopped. "The first to go was the kitchen table. It was round and made of oak. It had carved chairs. The biggest surprise was a nutmeg grater made of pewter, something Cody used to play with. He got me seven hundred dollars for it. Imagine that."

"That much for a nutmeg grater?"

"Yeah, but Uncle Boyd said it was very old. He sold the player piano and all the music rolls two weeks before I moved in with Pa. It was the one thing I wanted to keep. Cody used to laugh and laugh as the piano's keys moved up and down. Did your mother buy that, too?"

"No, she didn't."

"Oh, too bad."

Her storytelling was as plain as rough-sawn wood. She seemed pleased so far she could handle whatever came her way. Even when she got to the painful parts, like her daddy's sorrows or Cody's odd little ways, she talked without pity. Several times, Willi asked Miles to tell her what it was like to go to college, to live somewhere else, how he built with wood. He preferred listening to her stories. Both of their families lived here for generations, but they were separated by what they had. Early on, Miles's family-owned mills along the town's rivers while Willi's folks worked them. He's never gone

160

without, although he knew she has.

Willi leaned against him, her hand playing inside his.

"You looked like you were enjoying Dave's girls," Miles said. "I hope they didn't make you upset."

Her fingers fluttered like a small bird caught in his hand.

"Them? No. Besides, I've decided it's all right to cry sometimes. It means I miss my boy." Her eyes fastened on his. "I expect a part of me will always be permanently sad. I think you understand what I mean."

He squeezed her hand gently.

"Yes, I do."

At the Pine Tree

Miles locked the house. As he drove past the Pine Tree on the way back to Dave's sugarhouse to get her car, he asked if she wanted to stop for a beer. Feeding the firebox made him thirsty he told her. A few pickups were parked in the lot, and since it was getting close to last call, the place should be nearly empty.

He waited until Willi thought about it.

"I guess it'll be all right."

Miles parked the truck near the entrance to the snowmobile trail. The woods still had enough snow for the machines to travel, but that would change soon.

"You sure you want to do this?" Miles asked her.

She gave him a tentative smile.

"Why not?"

They walked to the line of stools at the bar, where the bartender greeted them. The waitress on duty ate her dinner on the other end of the counter. A couple of regulars played pool. One guy Miles knew from Tyler hung over the jukebox, making his selection.

"Shit, it'd better not be that song again," the bartender muttered as the man stumbled back to his table. "His girlfriend dumped him, and now we all have to suffer along with him listening to that stupid song."

The waitress stuffed a French fry in her mouth.

"No shit. He's been at it all night."

Willi hummed the tune, just another song about love gone bad. She didn't play an instrument, but Miles decided she had a natural ear. At the end, when the man stood, the bartender yelled, "Hey, you! Play that song one more time, and I'll pull the plug."

The man sat down. Willi giggled. Her laughter was as

pleasant as jingling coins, and Miles wanted to sustain it. He began telling her about the condition of the men's room, how they hooked a telephone cord through a hole where the knob should be to keep it shut, and the place stunk like cats had been trapped in there for a week. Willi laughed more when he told her about the hole in the floor.

"Wait. You should see the writing on the wall. If you believe any of it, the people of Hayward are committing some pretty unnatural acts."

Miles rested against the back of his stool. Every time Willi tried to speak, laughter spilled from her mouth and her shoulders shook. Her eyes were open wide and a little wet.

"Remember the time Dave and I saw you at the Penfield Fair? We were just kids, and you were hanging around with your friends under the stands. We were going to get Dave's cows ready for the 4-H ring, and your friends were drinking and smoking."

"Those kids. I think I asked if you wanted to join us."

"Yeah, but we felt like boys when we saw you and them."

"I should've offered you some liquor and made men out of you."

Miles started laughing.

"We thought you were so wild. Remember those cut-offs you were wearing?" he asked.

"No."

She didn't stop smiling

"Well, I sure do." He chuckled. "Wild Willi Merritt."

"Yup, that's me all right."

The door to the Pine Tree opened, and the bartender shouted to three men wearing snowmobile gear they had time for one round. Miles frowned when he saw Junior, his father, Joe, and his brother, Mike. He whispered that fact to Willi, who did a quick peek.

Mike Miller walked toward the bar to put his arm around the waitress.

"Then, you'd better bring us those three beers fast." He leaned over the bar. "Hey, check it out. If it isn't Willi Miller. What's a girl like you doing in a place like this?"

163

Willi fired him a hard look. "Shut up, Mike. Why don't you go home to your wife?" she said.

It was the waitress's turn to glare at Willi. Miles wondered how far this could go and what he might have to do to stop it.

"And who else do we have here? Miles Potter. Hey, I thought we told you to stay away from Willi." He turned toward his brother. "Right, Junior?"

Miles glanced at Junior, but he was silent. Joe Miller was at the table, taking it all in like it was a show.

"Mike, we don't want any trouble from you and your brother. Why don't you leave us alone?" Miles said.

"You hear that, Junior? He don't want any trouble. That's rich."

Miles felt a burn build inside him as deep and hot as the fire he tended all night. He shifted on his bar stool when Mike patted his shoulder. But then Junior called to his brother in a friendly way.

"Let's drink those beers," he said. "There's not much time left."

Junior gave Willi a hello, but her face was blank. She gave him a nod then stared ahead at the three long rows of liquor behind the bar.

Miles bent toward her. "Let's leave," he whispered.

Willi shook her head and drank from the bottle.

"They're not chasing us outta here."

"Okay, if that's what you want."

The three Miller men settled down when the bartender delivered their beers to the table. They got busy with the waitress, laughing at each other's jokes in loud drunken barks. Miles placed his hand on Willi's beneath the bar.

"Okay, I'm ready to go," she said.

Willi walked beside Miles with her head up, but she turned left when Junior's father called her name, then made a dirty cackle. He kissed the air.

She held Miles's arm, but he broke from her grasp as he marched toward the table. Mike and Joe jumped up, dumping bottles onto the floor. Mike shoved Miles, who pushed him back against his father, who began cursing at them all. The waitress yelled at them to stop. The bartender came fast from the backroom, but that was enough. Nobody wanted to get kicked out of the only bar in town.

Junior sat, not saying a word. He drank his beer and stared at Willi who waited near the door. Her face was pale, and Miles went to take her away.

What to Believe

By time Junior showed up for Marjorie's party the next night, Pop was half in the bag. Pop and Mike drank shots of Jim Beam and Bud from the bottle at the dining room table while Ray sat on the other side of the table, taking it all in while Lorna and Mike's wife, Dee, were busy in the kitchen. They were having cold cut sandwiches, potato salad, and Dee's baked beans. Lorna brought a decorated cake from the bakery.

Pop's wife, the birthday girl, wore a black, low-cut top, which showed off the freckled skin of her chest. She drank Amaretto, Junior's gift, but showed more restraint than her husband, who sat next to her making jokes at her expense.

"How old did you say you was, sweetheart? That old? Hee-hee, time to trade you in for a new model."

"What would a new model want with you?" she spat.

Marjorie let the smoke from her cigarette run through her nose, which gave Junior the impression she had caught fire. But Pop was in too fine of a drunk to take offense. His hand made loud slapping noises as it hit the clear vinyl cover over the lace tablecloth.

"Shit, honey, that's a good one." Pop gave her an exaggerated wink. "I'll be giving you my present later tonight, if you know what I mean."

She whacked him on the arm. "Shut up, Joe. You're embarrassing the kids."

"You mean Junior and Mike? I think I told 'em about that sort of thing. Hee-hee. Right, boys?"

Mike reached toward the radio on the hutch to turn up a Country and Western song. It was a catchy tune with lots of hard guitar playing and a man singing about honkytonks and women.

166

"Great song, eh, Junior?"

Mike stood up to dance, his legs shimmying and the toes of his cowboy boots moving this way and that.

Marjorie pointed and squealed. "Hey, Mike's dancing just like that singer, what's-his-name."

"Yeah, he looks like old what's-his-name all right," Junior quipped.

Mike's three boys ran around the house, bumping into furniture and tagging each other. Junior wondered how his boy would have fared with his cousins. He imagined Cody sticking close to his mother, watching them as if they were a storm passing through.

Junior was not used to the kids' commotion. But no one else seemed to mind, except their mother, who yelled occasionally from the kitchen.

Finally, Dee stuck her head through the doorway. "Jesus, Mike, can't you make 'em stop?"

In response, Mike shoved his lit butt between his lips as he yanked one kid's arm so hard he nearly fell to the floor. He threatened the other two, who stared with open mouths at their father.

Pop spoke up. "Aw, let the boys have fun. You wanna turn 'em into sissies?"

Dee threw up her hands and retreated to the kitchen. She was an attractive woman, but he bet his lamebrain brother only saw Dee as interference to his idea of fun. Wake up, Mike, he felt like telling his little brother. Don't throw this away. What girl's going to want you when you're old like Pop?

Junior finished his shot and slid his glass forward for Pop to fill, which he did gleefully, because he was happy to be drinking with his family. Besides, Pop was in a celebratory mood. His ankle had healed enough, so he could go back to work next week. He had stopped using his cane. "Vacation's over," he kept joking, but Junior knew his father was a man who couldn't stay put, especially after Marjorie canceled the dirty movie channel.

His head jerked up from his drink when his father called his name.

"Hey, Junior, what the hell's wrong with you today? Haven't seen you smile all night." He elbowed his middle son. "Hey, Mike, tell him that joke you told me, the one about the Siamese twins. Aw, never mind. I'll do it."

So, Pop began telling the joke, which Junior might have enjoyed more because it was really low, if he weren't distracted by the boys' restless noise. They were waiting for Willi, who called to say she was having a problem with her car. Ray, who came to the party as Lorna's guest, asked from his place at the dining room table whether she needed his help. But it appeared Wayne next door fixed whatever it was, so she was on her way.

Across the table, Ray nursed the first shot Pop poured him and he was only halfway through his first beer, a wise move on his part. Ray was a brave man to show his face here. He gave Marjorie, who he called Mrs. Miller, a gift certificate for a free oil change at his garage, which drew favorable comments from the men and a smile from the birthday girl.

Lorna warned them all before Ray's arrival they were to be on their best behavior. "Be nice, you bastards. I don't want you scaring him off. Do y'all understand?"

She said it so sternly even Pop didn't argue.

Junior was feeling a solid buzz when he heard Willi greet Lorna and Dee in the kitchen. She sped through the dining room, holding a wrapped gift and a shopping bag she set near the wall. Her eyes flitted from one person to another. She smiled tentatively as she said her hellos. Mike's boys surrounded Willi as she bent to hug each one.

He tried to picture himself in her place. At one point, her eyes met his, and he vowed to rescue her from any prying questions by these boys. But it wasn't necessary, as it appeared they had been told not to mention their dead cousin. No one else did. It was as if Cody was never a part of the family. It seemed as if he didn't ever live.

"My, you boys have grown," Willi told them.

The boys scattered when their mother and then Lorna came into the room. Marjorie, a little sloppy from the Amaretto, hit Lorna's arm. "Check out your sister with her hair done up like that."

Willi's blond hair was twisted into a knot on top of her head. It made her look as young as when Junior first met her, and it stirred familiar feelings for that girl. Willi handed her mother the gift, pecking her on the cheek. "This is from Lorna and me. Happy birthday, Mom."

Joe, who hadn't said a word since Willi arrived, pointed to his puckered lips and made smacking noises. "How about a little kiss for me?"

Mike laughed, but Junior could see it wasn't a joke for Willi, who glared at Pop.

"Don't hold your breath, Joe," Willi said.

Her mother frowned. "Willi, that's not very nice. I brought you up better than that."

Pop refilled their glasses. "Aw, leave her alone," he growled. "That's our Willi, our sweet, little Willi."

If Willi heard him, she said nothing. Instead, she sat next to Ray while Lorna bugged her mother to open the gift. Marjorie used a long, red fingernail to slice the tape. She made a rattle in her throat when she saw what was inside.

"Oh, girls, you remembered. It's the 'Jailhouse Rock' plate. For my collection." She stood to kiss Lorna and then stretched across the table for one from Willi. "Thank you, girls. See, Joe?"

But Pop watched Willi. His brow hung low, pushing his eyelids nearly shut. The way his father looked made Junior feel as if he'd come in the middle of something.

The Picture

After the food was brought to the table and everyone had fixed their plates, Willi pulled the framed picture of Cody from the shopping bag and went down the hallway to her mother's room. She wanted to put the photograph in its place without drawing anyone's attention. She flicked on the light and walked to the wall beside her mother's dresser to slip the frame on its hook.

Willi took a step backward. Someone at school had said the right thing to make her son happy, and for that instant, Cody was like other little boys.

She sighed deeply.

"There you are, sweetie."

Willi almost didn't come. After the incident at the Pine Tree, she dreaded it, but she didn't want to disappoint her mother or Lorna, who had planned this party for weeks. Then, there were Mike and Dee's boys. Cody wasn't close to his cousins, but they played together at the occasional family gathering. The boys enjoyed getting Cody wound up. She was sure they weren't being kind when they got her son to run around and make loud moans, but it saddened her when they didn't mention him tonight. Dee and Mike probably told the boys not to talk about Cody, so her feelings wouldn't get hurt. But she wouldn't have minded shedding a few tears, knowing they remembered him as their cousin.

She turned to her left when she heard a man clear his throat. Junior stood in the doorway.

"I didn't wanna scare you," he said. "You seemed kinda far away."

"I was."

She waited, worried about what he was going to say this time. In the other room, she heard a crash, some shouts, and then laughter.

"Sounds like things are getting outta control back there." Junior chuckled. "Ray was nuts to come, and Lorna was double-nuts to bring him. I bet he's thinking twice about hookin' up with her."

"I hope not. Lorna cares a lot about him."

Junior reached into his back pocket for his wallet. He pressed five twenties in Willi's hand. She looked at the money, and then Junior's face.

"Thanks, Junior. I need to get another car. Ray says mine is shot." She noticed he was listening to her carefully. "Ray wondered if Pa's old truck would be worth fixing. He's gonna check it out."

"You and Ray seemed pretty chummy back there."

"He's awfully nice to my sister. I like that."

Joe's voice rose above the others. He hollered for everyone to shut up. He wanted to make a toast to his wife. Willi needed to help Lorna get the cake ready, so she reached for the light switch in the bedroom but stopped when Junior spoke.

"I'm sorry about the other night at the Pine Tree. Mike can be a jerk when he drinks too much."

She turned toward Junior. "Does my mother know anythin' about that?"

"If she does, she's said nothin' to me." He took a step closer. "What are you doin' with Miles Potter anyway? You ain't sleeping with him, are you?"

She squeezed the bills tightly. "It's none of your business, Junior. We ain't married anymore."

Junior screwed up the features on his face. He opened his mouth, then shut it. When he turned and left the room, his boot heels clipped against the wooden floor.

Willi remained a few minutes to steady herself before she returned to the family. But in the hallway, Joe wobbled toward her. At first, she thought he walked like that because of his bad ankle, but he was plain drunk, so wasted he held onto the walls to keep from falling on his face. Willi stayed still, deciding whether to let Joe pass or to rush by him, but he came toward her faster than she could make the choice.

"Well, well, well, who do we have here?" She went forward, but he blocked her way. "Not so fast, sweetheart. That wasn't very nice what you said back there. Not nice at all. And we both know you and me go *way* back, don't we, honey?"

"Stay away from me."

Joe laughed as he grabbed her upper arm, pulling her near as she squirmed to break away. His mouth was so close she smelled his boozy breath.

"I can see why you married my boy. He's just like me." His free hand ran down the front of her blouse. "When I saw you with Miles Potter, I almost shit my pants. Jesus, Willi, he killed your kid."

She clenched her teeth. "Let me go, Joe."

His moan was a mean, dirty thing.

"Don't worry. I haven't told your Ma anythin' yet. But maybe I should." He pulled at her buttons. "That's right. I like it when you're scared of me. It's more fun that way."

Willi made a small cry when she pushed Joe as hard as she could, which really didn't take much to send him to the floor. "I told you not to touch me," she said.

Willi stepped past him, sprawled on the floor, but she didn't get too far because Ma was at one end of the hallway. When Willi glanced back, Junior was on the other, zipping his fly as he came from the toilet. Junior and Ma's faces twitched as Joe cursed and tried to get himself to his feet.

"Willi, what in the hell did you do to my husband?" her mother yelled.

Ma stooped to help Joe, but he made half-rolls on the floor, groping for Willi's ankles. Willi kicked his hand as she stomped away.

"Tell that drunk you call a husband to keep his hands to himself," she told her mother. "Next time, I'll fix him good."

Willi didn't stop. She rushed through the rest of the house to the kitchen where she grabbed her jacket and purse, and then out the back door. She was inside her car, locking the doors and praying the engine would catch. When she was finally able to drive away, her heart beat as dangerously as the click from the front wheel of her car.

Long Gone

Willi was long gone by time Junior and Mike got Pop back on his feet and back into the dining room without his hurting himself. It wasn't easy. Their old man kept fighting them off. Pop's voice cut like a chainsaw. "Go back and get that girl for me. I'm not done with her."

Junior tightened his grip on his father's arm.

"Jesus, Pop, you're really wasted," Mike said.

They planted Pop in his chair, although he almost fell to the floor when he tried to get up again. Pop reached for his shot glass, but Junior snatched it away. "That's enough for you tonight, Pop."

Mike's boys circled the room to get a better look at their grandfather, who was banging his fist on the table. "Get me another drink, boys. Where'd that Willi go?"

Marjorie frowned.

"Joe's right," she said. "Willi must be off her rocker. Well, she didn't get that from my side of the family. I can tell you that."

Junior felt like telling Marjorie to shut up. His old man had it coming. He saw what happened. Pop was lunging at Willi and trying to kiss her. He was feeling her up. The words "Hey, what are you doing" were forming in his mouth when his ex-wife took care of it herself.

He downed his drink. This was one doozy of a get-together, even by his family's standards. He wasn't going to come, but Pop insisted. He said they'd get drunk and wish Marjorie a happy birthday, but it didn't work out that way. Now, Pop made wet noises with his mouth. He looked as if he were going to fall asleep. Marjorie was still at it, bad-mouthing Willi. Lorna avoided her. Ray stared at whoever was speaking.

173

The poor slob should drive as fast as he can from this screwed-up family.

Junior poured himself and Mike another drink. It appeared things were settling down, but then one of Mike's boys dropped the Elvis plate, chipping its back. Dee slapped the kid on the butt and shrieked at Mike, who told her to shut up. Marjorie was wailing about the plate's lost value, and Lorna was ready to burst into tears. At that point, Junior wanted to fling the plate against the wall, so Elvis would smash into a hundred little pieces.

Lorna's boyfriend, Ray turned the plate over in his hand. "Gee, Mrs. Miller, it's only a little chip on the back. No one's going see it from the wall," he spoke in a deep, calm voice. "Elvis is as good as new."

Marjorie shot Ray a killer stare, but Lorna smiled gratefully at him as she went to get the cake.

Dee left with the boys after a half-hearted round of "Happy Birthday" and the cake was cut. Pop didn't touch his. He was passed out in his chair, listing heavily to the side, so he was in danger of falling to the floor. At some point Junior and Mike would have to steer Pop to the couch, so he could sleep it off. Marjorie eyed her husband, and then stuck her lit butt in the middle of her cake, which sent Lorna running to the kitchen. Ray left shortly afterward.

Later, in the truck, Mike said to Junior, "That was one fucked-up party. What in the hell happened back there with Willi?"

Junior watched the road. "I saw Pop grab Willi's tits. She gave him a push. I'm sorry to say Pop is a dirty old man."

Mike whistled.

"No wonder she's pissed. I mean, she flew out of the house. She didn't even say bye to Dee or Lorna." He didn't speak for a while. "Well, I's sure like to feel her up."

Junior gave Mike a hard shove. "Keep your hands off her if you know what's good for you."

"All right, all right, Junior." Mike rubbed his arm. "Hey, how about we go to the Pine Tree? I dunno about you, but I'm still in a party mood."

174

Junior took the next right. "I'm not. So, I'm gonna drop you off home. You can kiss your wife hello and read your kids bedtime stories."

"You're shittin' me."

Junior braked the truck.

"No, I'm not shittin' you. And I believe this is where you live."

Not Gone His Way

After Junior left Mike, he drove toward Dave's sugarhouse to check on Willi before he went to the Pine Tree Tavern. He slowed the truck, but Willi's junk wasn't there, he was glad to see, although he recognized Miles's truck. He never liked the man, but he knew he'd treat Willi better than he ever did. Junior shook his head. He'd call her when he got to the Pine Tree, just to make sure she was okay.

Junior reached for the pack of cigarettes on the dash. Things weren't going his way. Soon the guy with the fixed hernia would be back to work, so his job at Dexter Propane was likely through. He asked around town, but that turned up with zero possibilities of another. Willi was being stubborn about the lawsuit, and nothing was going to happen if she wouldn't go along with it. If Junior wanted to give her more money, he'd have to sell something, maybe his spare snowmobile. He was thinking of calling his kid brother, Dustin. A fresh start in Florida sounded pretty good right now.

Junior frowned as he lit a cigarette. He wasn't bad looking. It was easy to get women to like him. And he could handle a piece of equipment better than many men. But he fell short on the things that mattered to most, like sticking to your word.

At least he wasn't like his old man.

What did he say to Willi? *I like it when you're scared of me.* Something bad happened between those two. How could he have missed it?

Junior parked in front of the Pine Tree. He knew what was waiting inside: a few guys who would rather drink and play pool than go home. Some of them would try to make it with the waitress or any other willing woman who was there. None of them were Willi, and Willi was the only woman he had felt

176

the kind of love that should last a man a lifetime. Seeing her tonight, with her hair up and her fighting spirit, he remembered why. But she'd never take him back. He was sure. He could never fix the wrongs he did to her and Cody.

Junior stubbed the butt in the ashtray as he eyed the neon lights of the Pine Tree Tavern. It was like watching a TV rerun with his mother. You could still laugh at the funny parts, but the elements of surprise and satisfaction were gone. He pulled the key from the ignition. He had nothing better to do.

Tired of Hearing

Willi dragged the stained mattress through the living room when she heard the phone ring, and then Junior's voice on the machine. "You there, Willi? You okay? Your car didn't break down, did it?" but she didn't listen to the rest. His voice sounded like a song she once liked but was tired of hearing. She pulled the mattress through the kitchen door and over the dirt floor of the shed. She leaned it against the woodpile. Miles said he would take it to the dump and help her get a new one.

She heard Junior say, "Bye now," as she stepped back inside the house. Foxy got up from her spot near the woodstove.

"Yeah, it's him," she told the dog.

Willi returned to Cody's room to finish cleaning but stopped. A small pile lay on the striped ticking of the box spring. She recognized the key to the front door, plus a small pink ball, coins, a gold crayon, and a photo of Cody and Pa. Her son had hidden them there. His little treasures. She lifted the photo. Her boy, clutching a large, metal dump truck, smiled so hard she could see most of his teeth. It was taken at Christmas, their last one with Pa, and a real good one she remembered. Pa gave Willi his wife's brooch, the cameo she wore to his and Cody's funerals. He played his guitar, and she roasted a small turkey. She gave Pa a plaid cowboy shirt with piping she found in the dry goods store in Tyler. The dump truck was a gift to Cody from the both of them.

She sighed so deeply Foxy paced and whimpered.

She bent to pat the dog's head. "It's okay, girl."

The phone rang again. She heard Lorna's voice.

"Willi, pick up the goddamn phone," she hissed. "It's me, Lorna."

She went to the kitchen to take the call. "Lorna, what are you whisperin' for?"

"Ma might hear me. She's in her room and she's hopping mad. Joe's passed out on the couch. Everybody else took off."

Her sister started crying.

"Gee, Lorna, take it easy."

"No, I ain't gonna take it easy. I wanted the party to be nice for Ma, but it turned out to be such a mess. A bunch of drunks spoiled it. It got worse after you left. Mike's kids are such brats. One of them even chipped the Elvis plate. And then, there was that fight with you and Joe." Her breath stuttered. "You know what Ray said? 'Is your family always like that?' Oh, Willi, he's not gonna wanna be with me anymore after this."

"Oh, Lorna, of course, he will. He'll still like you." Willi paused. "Hey, why don't I go see him tomorrow at his garage? My car's just about ready to die anyway."

"You'd do that for me?"

"Course, I would, Lorna."

Her sister sniffed. "Can I ask you somethin'? What happened between you and Joe?"

Willi stayed silent as she weighed how much she should say.

"He got me in the hallway and grabbed my boobs. I pushed him away. He was so drunk he just fell over, and he couldn't get up."

Lorna made a small gasp. "You should hear what him and Ma are sayin' about you."

"I don't wanna know. Really. I don't care about Joe. And Ma sees what she wants to see. Don't you get that?"

"I dunno, Willi."

"That's okay. I still love you, Lorna."

Willi hung up the phone and went to the couch. She let the dog sit with her while she waited for Miles. She thought about calling Dave's house, but it was too late. Ruth was probably in bed, and she didn't want to bother her. She turned on the TV but only for the light and noise.

She thought about what she could tell Miles about her family. How they forgot all about Cody, except for Lorna. How her drunken stepfather came onto her, and her mother blamed her. She bet Miles's family never did anything like that. He came from people who read books and wanted their kids to do better than them.

Then, there was all that old stuff with Joe. What would Miles think?

She pulled her legs up and wrapped her arms around her knees as she remembered the time Joe got caught watching her take a shower, and how her mother almost found out then about him when she came into the bathroom. Willi tried to find something to cover herself after she heard her mother's loud voice say, "Joe, what in the hell you doin' in here?"

"I didn't know she was in here. Honest. I had to go real bad. I knocked, but nobody answered. I thought she was just warmin' up the water. Really, Marjorie."

Willi ran wrapped in a towel to her room. Ma and Joe were still going at it.

Later, Ma came in her room.

"We're getting a lock for the bathroom so that don't happen again." Ma's head turned toward the door to her room. "And one for here. You're fourteen. You're getting too big to run around without enough clothes on. We have a man livin' in the house. You should know better."

You should know better. That's how her mother put it. But she wasn't ungrateful. The locks didn't stop Joe, but it slowed him down.

She was sixteen when she sharpened one of her father's hunting knives until it could split paper. The next time Joe came to her, the last one, she pulled it out. He laughed at her until the knife sliced through his shirt to the skin over his belly. He bled from the cut.

She jabbed the air with the knife when she told him, "You come near me again, I'll cut lower, and I don't care if I kill you and I have to go to jail for the rest of my life."

Joe drove himself to the hospital and later told her mother another lie she believed.

It was midnight when Willi gave up waiting for Miles. She let the dog out briefly before she got ready for bed. She left the door unlocked and the outside light on for when Miles came later.

180

Wish

The next morning, Miles watched from Willi's bed as she tucked her blouse into her jeans. His face was heavy with whiskers, not quite a beard. "You have to go to work already?"

"Uh-huh, why don't you go back to sleep?"

Miles finished boiling sometime after three, and when he slipped into bed, he smelled of maple steam and smoke as he wrapped himself around her.

He patted the space beside him. She sat on the mattress.

"How was your mother's party?"

She swallowed. "Awful. Joe got really drunk and spoiled it as usual."

"What'd he do? Drop the cake on the floor?"

Miles grinned at his joke.

Willi glanced down at her hands. "No, I wish it was somethin' like that."

He used the tip of a finger to lift her chin. "Hey, what's the matter?"

"It's a long story."

"Go ahead. I'll listen to all of it."

She studied his face. She smiled sadly. He meant what he said. But was he ready to hear it? "I don't have time right now," she whispered.

"How about later at Dave's?"

She shook her head.

"I might not make it tonight. There's something wrong with my car, and I have to take it to Ray's garage before I go to work." She kissed him quickly. "Go back to sleep. Don't you worry about me."

Over Here

Minutes later, Ray gave a jovial, "Over here," when Willi called his name inside the garage. She picked her feet over car parts strewn on the concrete floor as she made her way toward Ray, hunched beneath the hood of a car.

"Hey, there, Willi, what can I do for you today?" Ray said in his soft, slow way.

"I'm afraid my car has a new noise."

"Uh-huh, CV-joint's shot. Heard the click-click when you pulled in. That's not good, I'm afraid, considering your car's other problems. I hope you're not plannin' any trips."

She shook her head.

"No, no trips, just to work and back home," she said. "How long do you think my car can last?"

"Hard to say. Could go today or a couple of weeks. It's somethin' you need to take care of, though. It ain't safe to drive."

No wonder her sister loved Ray. She felt calmed even when he told her bad news. Willi leaned her elbow on the car's fender, studying the engine as if she could tell what was wrong with it. She was choosing her words, and Ray appeared content to wait in her silence.

"That was really bad last night, wasn't it? Lorna feels just awful about it. She wanted the party to be extra special for our mother. That's why she asked you to come." She sighed. "But with Joe's family, everythin' goes wrong."

He murmured as he pushed his oil-stained fingers through his hair. "Well, they didn't chase me away from Lorna if that's what you're worried about."

Ray pulled his mouth into a wide grin. Willi felt an ache. Theirs was a first love so new and straight ahead she might

182

feel jealous if it were happening to another woman and not her sister. She wasted her first love on Junior.

"You knew my grandfather. When we were growin' up, do you remember my Daddy? He was a little like you, quiet and gentle," she said, pleased that he followed her words carefully. "I think you're a good influence on my sister."

Ray's helper, a kid from town, rolled a tire across the floor. Ray's eyes followed him briefly before they returned to Willi. His head rocked slowly.

"I think I can bring the flatbed to your house Sunday to get your grandfather's truck," he said. "No promises, but I'll see if we can get her working again. Those old trucks are hard to kill." He grinned again. "Say, I'll bring Lorna with me if you like."

Willi smiled.

"Yeah, I would, and thank you."

A Hammering Heart

Willi was having a busy day at the Lucky Lady. It seemed every woman who sat in her chair wanted to have their hair rinsed blue or permed. Theresa said it must be old lady day but not so lucky lady day since they were such poor tippers. Willi would have liked the extra money, but she enjoyed making these women feel as if they were still pretty. Mrs. Henderson, her third-grade teacher, was her last customer. The woman watched her reflection in the mirror as Willi cut her hair. She was Willi's favorite teacher, because she had read aloud to them.

Willi used a blow dryer to finish the style. "Here, take a look," she said.

She handed the woman a mirror and spun her chair in a half circle.

"You do that well," Mrs. Henderson finally said. "Tell me, dear, how are you doing?"

She thought of Miles.

"Better, Mrs. Henderson."

"I'm glad to hear that. I would say you've had more than your share of trouble," she said. "You deserve better. I saw you with your boy. You were a caring mother to him."

"Thanks," she whispered.

Afterward, Willi cleaned her station. She gathered her coat and told Theresa good-bye before she headed to the Chuck Wagon to order a chicken sandwich and coffee to go. She was going home to feed Foxy before she went to Dave's sugarhouse to be with Miles.

The redheaded waitress placed the white slip with her order on the wide sill of the kitchen window. Her finger pressed the small chrome bell.

"This'll take a few minutes, honey. Why don't you sit down?"

184

Willi turned away. The restaurant, set to close soon, was empty except for Ma, Joe, and Junior, who sat in the back booth. Joe and Junior had their backs to her. Ma's face was pinched as she stared straight ahead and puffed a cigarette.

If Ma saw Willi, she pretended she didn't. Of course, her mother knew she was here. How could she not? She was the only other customer in the place. That made Willi sad and mad at the same time. Ma called Theresa this morning to say she wouldn't be coming to the Lucky Lady any more. Ma told Theresa to ask Willi why, but she only shrugged. "She's pissed at me for somethin' that's not my fault," she told her.

Her mother took a deep drag on her cigarette and blew it out again.

Willi stepped quickly across the restaurant and slipped into the booth's bench beside her mother. Ma's eyes drew crack-tight. Willi shot a glance at Junior, who told her hello, and Joe, who said nothing, but scowled. Willi took a deep breath.

"Ma?"

"What do you want, Willi?"

"I wanna talk about last night."

"What's there to talk about?" Ma nodded at Joe. "You shoved my husband to the floor. You spoiled my party."

"You're tellin' me you don't believe that he grabbed me first?"

Willi's head jerked toward Joe, who was working something inside his mouth.

"Yeah, I'm sayin' I didn't." Ma stomped the cigarette into her plate. She kept at it although the butt was out. "Your problem is you never liked Joe from the time I brought him home. You're such a selfish daughter."

That's what Ma used to say even before she met Joe.

"That's not true, Ma. I'm a good daughter. I've always been."

"And another thing." Her mother wagged her finger like it was overheated. "I heard about you and Miles Potter. Joe seen you at the Pine Tree. How long you think it's gonna last after he's done feeling sorry for you?" She snorted. "He'll drop you like a hot potato when he's done with you."

185

Her mother's laughter was small and hard.

"Ma, that's a mean thing to say. You dunno what you're talkin' about. That's not gonna happen."

Joe slammed his fist on the table.

"Shut ya mouth, girl. You make me sick." His voice was low and rusty. "First holdin' out about the insurance money. Then, my Junior wanted to sue that bastard. You could've gotten a bundle. You and my boy. But you didn't wanna do that." His eyes got smaller. "Then, there's all this crap you're sayin' about me. Getting your sister worked up." He sneered. "You could show a little gratitude for me and your mother for all we've done for you."

Willi's heart beat as if someone hammered the roof. She remembered how she felt when Joe was near, praying he'd just leave her alone. She glanced around the place. A teenaged boy was at the counter filling catsup bottles. This time Joe was not getting away with it.

She hissed, "All you've done for me? Why don't you tell my mother all the things you've done for me? Tell her about the times you got me alone when she wasn't around. What you made me do. Awful things. How you threatened me if I told Ma. How about tellin' her how you got that knife cut on your belly? You tell her the real story? How I did it the last time you came after me? No? Didn't think so."

Ma's head trembled as it spun toward the window.

Spit flew from Joe's mouth. "You lyin' little bitch."

"Shut up, Pop." It was Junior. His voice was low and forceful. "I saw what happened last night. What else you do to her?"

"I didn't do nothin'."

"Yeah, you did. I know you did. Jesus, Pop, she was just a little girl."

The double-chime of the bell rang. The waitress placed a white bag and a Styrofoam cup on the counter before she went back inside the kitchen. Willi's fingers shook as she brought them to her mouth. She wasn't going to let them see her cry.

"Ma, you gotta believe me."

Willi looked at her mother, still faced away, then Joe. His

186

eyes were small and sharp as he stared at her and then his son. She pressed her hand lightly on Junior's shoulder before she went to the front of the restaurant to get her order. She heard boot heels clack behind her.

"Willi, wait up." The voice came from Junior. But she was out the door and walking fast to her car. "Stop, I wanna talk to you."

The hinge ground metal as Willi yanked the door open. She slid into the front seat, putting the cup and white bag beside her. She dug inside her purse for the keys while she reached for the door, but Junior held it open.

"Let me go, Junior."

"Not until you answer me somethin'."

She jabbed the key into the ignition. "What is it Junior? What do you wanna say?"

"Why didn't you tell me about Pop?"

She wiped tears from each eye. "I didn't tell anybody. I couldn't. I was too ashamed."

Junior winced. "Aw, Willi, you shouldn't have kept somethin' like that to yourself. Not from the people who love you."

"And what would you have done if I told you? My own mother doesn't even believe me. You saw her. Besides, I don't think she loves me all that much."

He blew air in one soft whistle.

"You gonna see Miles? Yeah, you are. I drive by the sugar shack at night and I see your car there, Willi."

She gave the car a little gas when the engine sounded as if it was ready to stall. Junior held the door.

"Don't go yet, Willi. What are you gonna do with Cody's ashes?"

She grabbed the steering wheel. She glanced toward the restaurant, but her mother and Joe were still inside.

"I'd like to bury Cody next to Pop and Daddy. That'd be a good place for him, don't you think? I'd feel they were watching over him. I know that's silly, but I wanna believe it." She pressed her lips. "I wanna get him a stone, too. Something small."

Junior took off his cowboy hat. His eyes were soft as he tipped his head.

"I'd like to do that for our boy, if you don't mind."

She nodded. "That'd be real nice, Junior, real nice."

"Okay," he whispered.

"By the way, thanks for stickin' up for me in there." Her hand was on the shifter. "I gotta go. Really."

Junior shut the door. She put the car in drive. When she glanced in the rear-view mirror, he hadn't moved from that spot. He just stood there, rolling his hat in his hands.

Sugar Shack

Willi sat alone in Dave's sugar shack with only the hanging bulb over the entryway lit. No one was here or at Dave's house. The evaporator's stove was cold, so she kept on her jacket and dug her hands deep inside its pockets. She was glad for her new boots.

She paced, and then sat again, saw the radio, but left it alone. She remembered the food she bought at Chuck's and then forgot it.

Willi just kept thinking about what happened in the restaurant. What did Ma say? *How long you think that's gonna last after he's done feeling sorry for you?* Ma laughed at her. She didn't want to listen to anything she had to say about Joe. Willi frowned. Ma should've done better than that. Joe? Joe can go to the hottest part of hell.

She knew she'd have to talk with Lorna. It wouldn't be easy. Ma was different with Lorna. So was Joe. But her sister would believe her.

She had to tell Miles. Junior was right. It's why she came.

Willi stood when she heard the sap truck's engine strain with its load. She went outside, and Miles was alone. He was all-smiles as he jumped from the truck's cab. His kiss was quick and playful.

"Hey, you came after all." He reached for the leather gloves on the dash. "Just me today. Dave took Ruth to the hospital. Her water broke right near the evaporator. You should've seen Dave go nuts. Ruth was calmer than him, and she's the one having the baby. She even had to remind him to tie his boots."

"When did they leave?"

"Sometime around noon. Ruth's mother has the girls. I've heard nothing yet. I'm way behind today, so I'll be here most of the night, I'm afraid. Want to help?"

Willi nodded.

"Good. I'll show you how to fill the firebox. We might have some old work clothes around here, so you don't ruin what you have on. They'll be kind of big on you though. Hope you don't mind."

She followed him inside the sugar shack. He switched on all the lights and then went for the side shed. She placed her hand on his arm. "Miles, wait. I have somethin' to tell you. It's important."

His eyes swung toward her. He took off his gloves. "What is it, Willi?"

She sat on the wooden bench. Miles dropped beside her. She took a deep breath.

"When I was twelve, my mother married Joe," she began.

"Willi, go ahead. I'm listening."

The Weight

That night Junior walked toward his father's house as Lorna came out. She stopped short when she saw him in the porch light. She dropped a bag.

"Hey, Lorna, what's the rush?"

"I'm gonna see Ray." She tossed her head back toward the house. "I wouldn't go in there if I was you. Somethin' bad's goin' on. I'm not sticking around."

"What?"

"I came home and broken glass was all over the kitchen floor. Ma was lyin' down in her bedroom in the dark. I kept askin' and she wouldn't tell me. All she said was 'Go someplace else' and then she rolled over on her side."

"Pop inside?"

"He's in the living room with a bottle. Didn't look like it would take too much to set him off. So, I swept up the glass and grabbed my things. You know anythin' about it?"

He paused, deciding what he could say. Really, it was up to Willi to tell her sister. But she should hear what kind of man he was.

"Yeah, Willi had a big fight with Pop and your mother. It was at the Chuck Wagon. I was there. But you should talk with Willi about it." The spit inside his cheek made a clicking noise. "Uh-huh, that's what you should do."

"You're not gonna tell me?"

"Nah, it's not for me to say."

Lorna bent for her bags. "Where is she now? I tried callin' her."

"Probably with Miles Potter. She ain't sleeping with him, is she?"

Lorna screwed up the features in her face. "None of your business. You lost that right a long time ago."

191

"Yeah, well, I didn't see him hanging around Willi when she had Cody with her."

"Gee, neither did you, Junior."

Junior watched Lorna bring her bag to the rear of her car and then lift the lid of the trunk. He was going to help but decided not. Sometimes this sister thing really pissed him off. He walked into the house. Pop was sitting in the dark with a bottle between his legs. Deep, red scratches ran along one cheek. The TV was on, but he wasn't paying any attention.

Pop made wet noises with his mouth. His eyelids were heavy as if he was falling asleep. "What the hell you doin' here, boy?"

"Jesus, Pop, you look like hell."

"Where is she?"

"Lorna?"

"No, Marjorie."

"She's in the bedroom."

"Yeah, well, I think I just got fucked real bad. Thanks a lot, Junior."

"What do you mean thanks a lot? Seems to me like you didn't need my help for that." Junior's voice broke. "Jesus, you doin' that stuff to Willi. What kinda man are you?"

Pop cracked his bloodshot eyes. "If that's why you came, you might as well get the hell outta my house. In fact, why don't you just go back to New Hampshire or wherever you was before. I sure as hell don't need somebody like you around tellin' me what to do."

"That's fine by me, Pop. But just so you know how I stand. You disgust me, old man."

Sweet Trees

The next afternoon, Willi was a few miles from home when her car died along Route 133. The engine kept working but not the wheels except for the roll still left in them. She knew what was happening. Her rust bucket, as predicted by Ray, had met its end. She steered the car onto the road's shoulder.

She got out to lift the hood, but dropped it after she studied the engine. Its parts labored in loud, irregular movements like the innards of an old man's chest. What did she know about cars? Nothing, so she returned to the front seat and turned the key. She had to call Ray to send his wrecker for her car and figure a way to get to work tomorrow. Maybe Miles would offer his truck. Or Lorna could help.

"I guess that's that."

Willi opened her purse for a pen and a piece of paper to leave a note on the windshield. She didn't want someone thinking she'd fallen or thrown herself into the Mercy River, which now flowed in a boil beside the road. She wrote on the back of an envelope, "CAR BROKE DOWN. WALKING HOME. WILLI."

She checked her watch. It was at that point in the year when she was surprised the sun shined so brightly. She got out of work early when her last appointment canceled. A few cars and pickups passed, but to all but one driver, a guy she didn't know who offered her a ride, she was a casual walker on the road, not someone whose car didn't work.

Willi kept her jacket unzipped as her sneakers splashed over the rivulets of melted snow. She was happy to stretch her legs, happy about some things. She and Miles: That was a good thing. After she told him about Joe, he was ready to find the man or call the police until Willi begged him not to. Then, he said, "No one will ever bother you again."

She hadn't heard from Ma. It'd been a week. She wondered if she ever would. Lorna said Ma wouldn't talk about her, although one night she and Joe had a big fight. Lorna asked Willi what happened. "Come see me, Lorna, and I'll tell you why" is what she told her sister.

Willi stopped beside the road. The last time she stood here was when Miles tried to save her son. He was bent over her boy, breathing into his mouth, working to get his heart going. Her boy's hands stretched over the snowy road. The impact had pulled the mittens off his hands, but not the clips holding them to his sleeves. She bent to tug the mittens back on, so his hands wouldn't get cold.

The falling snow that day silenced everything but a steady yell inside her. She closed her eyes and heard it still, although fainter.

"Cody," she whispered.

Snow on large sections of the hill had melted, so she could no longer tell the exact way her son's sled had gone.

She came finally to the bottom of the hill on Barker Road. Maple trees flanked her walk, each holding gray metal buckets, so it seemed as if they had bulging pockets. The doctor was crazy about those buckets, insisting they use the sap they collected, even if it slowed them. Shane Buell complained, but Dave went along with it, driving his farm truck stop-and-go along the road while the kid leaped up and down from the bed to fetch the buckets of raw sap.

The vat at the bottom of the doctor's hill was nearly full. Dave would be here soon. They were midway through the season. The syrup they boiled was dark amber, still fine but a lower grade. The best syrup was already sealed in plastic jugs. Miles would likely be up again all night helping Dave. Ruth came home from the hospital with another redheaded daughter. Willi got to hold the girl they named Sarah. She was perfect.

Willi stepped into the driveway. Foxy sat on the shrunken snowbank next to Miles's pickup and made friendly barking riffs as she trotted toward her. A length of chain dangled from her collar. The dog had worked herself free, and Willi wondered what mischief she'd been up to at the doctor's.

"What am I gonna do with you?" she told the dog.

Willi unclipped the fragment of chain. She'd get the pliers from Pa's toolbox in the shed to fix it. She stopped and took in the land behind her house. The snow was getting thinner, so now large sections were bare to the frozen ground, and from this view, the Mercy River was dark blue. She eyed the brown grass where Pa's pickup used to park, hopeful Ray could fix it.

The dog followed her through the shed to inside the house to her bedroom, turning then dropping at the foot of the bed. Miles was still asleep. She stood in the doorway watching him breathe. He came this morning as she was going to work, kissing her before he settled into her warm sheets.

Miles opened one eye, then the other.

"Willi, you're home. Is it really that late?"

Willi dropped her sneakers on the floor and got beneath the covers beside Miles, laying her head against his chest, listening to the steady pump of his heart. She closed her eyes and smiled. She thought of nothing else.

Fantastic Books
Great Authors

- Gripping Thrillers
- Cosy Mysteries
- Romantic Chick-Lit
- Fascinating Historicals
- Exciting Fantasy
- Young Adult
- Non-Fiction

Discover us online
www.darkstroke.com

Find us on instagram:
www.instagram.com/darkstrokebooks

Made in the USA
Middletown, DE
27 September 2023

39063559R00120